Be My Angel

Dani Haviland

USA Today Bestselling Author

Be My Angel is a work of fiction. Names, place, characters, and incidents are the product of the author's imagination and are used for the readers' enjoyment. Any resemblance to persons living, dead, or fictional, events or business establishments is entirely coincidental.

Book Description

Wyatt had always been known as Big Jake's son, hot Colton's little brother, or the gawky stutterer. Now, relocating to new part of Oregon, he hopes to create his own identity while helping save wild American mustangs. When he finds an angel to help him pursue his dream, he doesn't want to let her go.

Acknowledgment

First, thanks for the inspiration, real Ashley! Keep on being strong!

I'd like to thank Lise Madson and Adopt Oregon Mustangs: Wild, Gentle & Trained for her extensive lists of links with information about the Bureau of Land Management programs for adopting mustangs, America's wild horses.
(https://www.facebook.com/pg/AdoptOregonMustangs)

I'd also like to thank Florine Kreeb for letting me borrow her first name for Grandma; Cousin Bella Conner, Victoria Zumbrum, and Heidi Lynn for the name Wyatt; Joelle Beebe, Kathleen O'Donnell and Rachael Aldridge for the name Colton; and long-time best friend Mona Pruett for the name Tucker.

Chapter One
I Fall Down, I Get Up

Thunk!

"Not again!"

Ashley stifled the curse that came to mind, just in case someone was standing nearby. As many times as she fell, you'd think someone would rush to her side. *Yeah, right, as if you'd let them help you up. Besides, no one can see you in this overgrown drainage ditch.*

Glad that she still had her gloves on, Ashley grabbed the prickly blackberry bush stringer and pulled herself up. However, gloves didn't help her arms. She wore long sleeved shirts, even in the summer, to try and keep down the scrapes and scratches from her frequent tumbles, but blackberry brambles were merciless. Still, she was better off than most people with cerebral palsy. At least she could walk unassisted.

Being born with cerebral palsy had been both the curse her mother indirectly bestowed upon her and the way she was able to be blessed by her determined no-nonsense grandmother.

"It's not your fault your mother used drugs and drank herself into a stupor, causing your premature birth. If I had been around or even known she was pregnant, I would have found her and locked her in her room to keep her clean, but she was long gone by that time. I hadn't heard from her in over a year when the labor and delivery room nurse called me. Shoot, I was there so quick, I didn't even change out of my mud boots."

Ashley grinned in recollection of the story she'd heard so many times. Grandma practically lived in those mud boots. She had to. The paths to the critter corrals on their little urban farm in Oregon were either muddy or dusty, depending on the time of year. Since she had been born in the middle of a particularly warm and wet winter, Grandma's boots were sure to have been covered in fresh mud.

"She had an easy labor, the doctor told me," Grandma had said. "She pushed you out without much effort at all because you were so tiny— just shy of three pounds. She was obviously high, so they tested both of you. Both tests came out positive. She couldn't say when she got pregnant, and she never had any pre-natal care, but it appeared you were at least two months early. She said she couldn't take care of you. If I didn't want to keep you, then she'd put you up for adoption. She didn't know your father. Or so she said. I think she was protecting someone by her shift of focus when she said, 'your father.'

"Of course, I wanted you. Who wouldn't? Or at least, who wouldn't if she was in her right mind? Don't hate your birth mother. She was, and is, in a bad place. Until she changes her focus from doing what feels good to her to what is right for her, she'll be more of a cripple than you could ever fear being.

"You were so tiny! The nurses warned me that you'd be developmentally delayed because you were a preemie. You were nearly a year old, though, before the doctor confirmed that there was something wrong with you. I knew you should be able to sit up and at least roll across the floor by ten months, but you didn't have any muscle tone. You could barely swat at the little ponies on your mobile that floated above your head in the crib, but you tried. You were challenged by what life had dealt you, but I could also see you were very determined."

Grandma wiped her eyes, then continued. "That was the

only thing that kept your attention: those bright pink and purple toy ponies. I'd untie one and set you on the floor on your belly, urging you to crawl to it. You'd try and try, but you just didn't have the strength. That's when I sought out a specialist. I had you working out with resistance bands years before it was a popular body building technique. You'd be an invalid if I hadn't."

Ashley pulled off a clinging piece of blackberry vine and continued walking to the horse corral up the road, her gait awkward but determined. It was the first sunny day in months and she had a bag of wrinkled apples in her backpack, The Prince's favorite snack. Time for training to get serious again.

Chapter Two
Off to School I Go

Beep! Beep!

Ashley pushed the button on her scooter, warning the foot traffic that she was coming through. You'd think that between the bright orange flag on the six-foot fiberglass pole attached to the homemade Fred Flintstone-style cab painted pink that covered her ruby-red powered wheelchair she would be visible enough to keep other students from running into her, but it wasn't always enough. All that too many of them saw was their smartphone in front of their faces, and maybe a backpack ahead of them. Side traffic was invisible. Most of the other community college students were in their late teens or early twenties and agile, every one of them in a hurry for one reason or another.

I wish I was in a hurry to go somewhere or see someone special! Today is Tuesday, so it will be another boring lecture on leadership development. As if I'll ever be in a managerial position! All I want to do is get my animal husbandry degree, whether I use it or not.

"Excuse me," Ashley said, waiting for the man in blue jeans and checkered Western shirt to move away from the classroom door.

When he didn't budge, she honked the horn on her scooter, and said even louder, "Excuse me, sir. I need to get into this room."

The dark-haired man turned half-way around to let Ashley see he was helping an elderly woman with a walker negotiate the doorway to leave the room.

"Oops! Sorry," Ashley said, then looked behind her and backed up, affording the gray-haired senior full access to the hallway. *You're not the only special needs person at this college, woman! At least be a little considerate, Ashley!*

As soon as the gracious senior was safely on her way, shuffling down the hall, the dark-haired hatless cowboy gestured wide, his arm held out, showing Ashley the way was clear to enter the classroom.

"Thank you," she said, making sure she enunciated her words. She maneuvered her red ride into her usual place: the corner by the window where it was out of the way, but where she could still see the whiteboard if the instructor wrote out an assignment.

That new guy's cute! And polite! Maybe he'll think you just twisted your ankle and borrowed the scooter until it healed. Ashley snorted and shook her head. *Fat chance of that! Well, at least when you're riding, you have a zero chance of falling down and really embarrassing yourself!*

She was wrong: the lecture on leadership wasn't boring. The substitute teacher had the most magnetic personality she'd ever seen. The whole classroom followed the handsome man's every movement, like they were metal shavings and he was a giant horseshoe magnet.

"It's your attitude more than your physical appearance or knowledge that commands followers," the guest instructor said. "I could be standing in front of you, wearing a ball gown, offering you the key to winning the Irish Sweepstakes, but if I was hunched over like this," the thirty-ish dark haired speaker hung his head low, crowded his shoulders together in classic submission attitude, then spoke softly, "would you pay any attention to me?"

He widened his shoulders and stood tall, then stuck his chin out and boomed, "But would you like to hear about the ABCs?" he asked boldly. "A is for Appaloosa, a fabulous breed of horse." He stepped forward, his right arm sweeping across the room, adding to his commanding voice with bold body language. "Now, would you like to hear about B?"

"Yeah, yeah!" the class replied, excited by the sudden change in attitude by the beguiling orator.

He returned to his former meek stature. "Well, B is for boring. And that's what you'll be if you speak soft like this." He sighed, disinterested in his own voice, "Or when you approach your topic like this," he bent his head down and shuffled forward.

The whole class roared with laughs and guffaws, one student saying, "I wish I'd recorded this for YouTube!"

The lecture continued, not a yawn or head nodding in boredom as the teacher captured the attention of the diverse class, males and females alike grinning, eyes sparkling, as if their favorite movie star had graced their classroom.

"So, if there is nothing more you learn from attending college, make sure that whatever it is you have to say or share, you do it with conviction. Attitude is everything. Thanks for being here today. Your regular teacher will return next week."

The guest lecturer picked up his notes from the podium, put them in his brown leather briefcase, then headed toward the door, the class standing and waiting to follow him as he left.

It looks like both the guys and the gals have crushes on him! He's cute and commanding, but as he said, it's all about attitude. He probably hates animals.

Ashley held back, waiting for the crowd to thin before she made her way to the door. She glanced down at her watch. Eleven o'clock. Her stomach said it was noon. Of course, by the time she made it out of the building and down the street to the Dairy Barn, it would be lunch time.

Might as well get started. She turned the key, powering up the electric scooter, and twisted the handle forward, making her way to the back of the flock of admirers. Suddenly, they moved out the door, following the speaker into the hallway like he was a rock star.

And there he was again, the other new face she'd seen today. Her hatless cowboy was holding the door open for her egress. "Thank you," she said, smiling with genuine appreciation.

He did it! He made eye contact! He didn't look off into the distance, with a 'My mama said to be kind to old folks and cripples' attitude. It was a genuine smile, like he was a nice person, glad to be able to help me.

Wyatt nodded at the young woman on the red scooter. He didn't like to flirt like his older brother did continually, but right now, he couldn't help himself. He pointed to the top of the homemade cover that shielded the rider from the elements, then cocked his thumb like he was shooting at the roof, wordlessly letting her know he thought it was cool.

"I like my ride, too," Ashley said, then headed out of the building, her sunny smile undeterred by the pouring rain outside. "And I think you're pretty cute, too," she whispered.

***

"I'll have a number one with a root beer," Ashley said, waiting for the clerk to acknowledge her.

"Oh, I'm sorry. I didn't see you there," the perky blonde attendant said. "You said a number one?"

"Yes, please."

"And what did you want to drink with that?" Blondie asked, her eyes focused on the person behind Ashley.

"Root. Beer. Please," Ashley answered, holding back the rage that always came unbidden when she was treated like an invisible entity.

"All right. Here's your number," she shoved the plastic

table number to Ashley, then looked up and said, "May I have your order, please," eyelashes aflutter, addressing the person behind Ashley.

"Don't you want to get paid, or is it feed the cripples for free day?" Ashley asked, not even trying to hide her bitterness.

"Oh, shoot! I'm so sorry," Blondie said, and took the five-dollar bill. She finished ringing up the transaction, then handed Ashley the paid receipt. She looked her in the eye. "Really. I am sorry. Truly."

Ashley palmed the slip of paper into her curled fist and shrugged one shoulder. "Sure," she mumbled, then maneuvered the scooter to the table in the corner that didn't have a chair in front of it. Her spot. Every Tuesday and Thursday around noon, except in the summer when she didn't go to school spot. The cripples' corner.

Wyatt was embarrassed for both the server and patron. He'd seen it too many times in his life, but he couldn't do anything about it except not to repeat the offense. He stepped aside and let the frowning female ride over to the table with the blue handicapped emblem emblazoned above the wall. Another unintentional stigma.

He took a deep breath, looked up at the backlit menu, and held up one finger.

"Will that be a number one for you, sir?" Blondie asked.

He replied with a nod, then pointed to Little Miss Scooter Rider.

"Oh, and a root beer for you, too?" she asked.

He nodded again, handed her a fiver, then accepted the plastic number she handed him.

Be bold! Go ahead and sit next to her. What's the worst she could do? Ask you to leave? Slap your face? Nah, she'd have to reach up too high to do that. Wyatt shook his head, ashamed at himself. Again.

Timidity won once more.

Wyatt sat at the table next to the handicapped spot, close enough that he could be in her presence, but far enough away that he wasn't invading 'her space.' He pulled out his smartphone and watched the sine waves on the graphs. All in the normal range. He switched screens and pulled up a solitaire game in progress. Diversion always worked to calm his muscles. Boring routines and repetitive movements were his friends.

"Well, you two made it easy for me," Blondie said as she

brought out one tray with both drinks and burgers. "The only thing easier would be if you were at the same table."

Wyatt gave a soft laugh, then stood up and moved one table over before he could doubt himself. "Better?" he asked, then realized what he had just done.

"Sure," Ashley said, then blushed scarlet. She dropped her head and grabbed the straw, awkwardly struggling to get the paper off it. The harder she tried, the clumsier her hands became.

She has purpose stress! Wyatt took the straw that had flipped out of her hand onto the table, set it aside, then unwrapped his straw and stuck it into her drink, scooting the cup close to her. *Oh, how I wish I could just say, 'Here you go,' without freaking out!*

"Thanks," Ashley said, then leaned forward and took a long drink. She really wasn't that thirsty, but she wouldn't have to say anything with the straw in her mouth.

Cool! She's polite but not too chatty.

Wyatt took the mangled straw and set it aside. He popped the lid off his drink and took a long straw-less draught. He wiped the back of his hand across his root beer mustache and smiled, resisting the urge to wink. That would be too over the top.

Ashley couldn't believe she was having lunch with this cute guy. And what a sense of humor on top of being a gentleman! She'd never felt this comfortable around a male who was her age. Shoot! Even other women the same age made her feel self-conscious about her disability. She picked up her burger and peeled back the wrapper. Or tried to. Suddenly, her hands were on strike. She slapped at the napkin, grasping it at the same time, then slid her mayo-painted hand into her lap.

"H-h-here," Wyatt stuttered, then partially unwrapped and re-wrapped the burger, offering it to her, ready for her to eat without dribbles or drips.

"Wow! Thanks," Ashley said, then took a bigger bite than she had expected. *He's cute but not perfect. That's why he doesn't talk: he has a stutter! Cool! His mouth stutters and my hands stammer. We'd make a cool couple.*

The two ate in a comfortable silence. Wyatt, glad that his secret stutter had been revealed in a casual setting; Ashley, glad that she was eating with a guy, any guy, but especially a nice one who didn't appear to be trying to borrow money or sell her something.

"You know, I can walk. I don't need the scooter all the time, but when I'm at school or crossing busy streets, I feel safer. It's embarrassing when I fall down." She paused, rolled her eyes, then pulled up the sleeve on her jacket, revealing a multitude of scrapes and scratches in various stages of healing. "And I fall down a lot."

Wyatt reached out and held her outstretched hand. "I used to, too."

He dropped her hand, realizing that he had essentially just made a pass at her, but that he had also spoken to her without a stutter.

"Really?" Ashley asked, oblivious of his combination grand faux pas and success. "You used to fall down a lot, too?"

"Y-y-yes," he said, then looked sideways, trying to figure out whether he should see if he should hold her hand again or not. *Look into her eyes! She wants you to! She's not mad.*

Wyatt gently covered her hand with his. "I have Dystonia," he said, then smiled. "And I stutter." His mouth worked back and forth, trying to calm his wide grin. "But I don't stutter when I hold your hand." He let go of her hand. "L-l-look!"

Both of them started laughing. Ashley took his hand this time. "So, tell me, what's your name? Oh, I'm Ashley, by the way."

"Ashley By the Way, I'm Wyatt. You met my brother earlier. He was the substitute teacher for your leadership class. Wow! I've never talked this much without a stutter."

"You do know that By the Way is not really my last name, right?" Ashley teased, then realized that this was the first time she had ever flirted. Bantering words with surrogate grandpas and uncles didn't count.

Wyatt nodded, then realized he could talk. "I think I'll have to get to know you better. I think you must be an angel, not an Ashley."

"Are you a cowboy?" Ashley asked, intentionally ignoring his angel remark. That's what Grandma had always called her, and she didn't want to think about Wyatt and Grandma at the same time.

"Oh, you mean the jeans, boots and shirt?" Wyatt asked, looking down at the snap closures on his light blue plaid shirt. "Yup. Well, not so much cows as horses. I've never ridden a cow, just a horse. Our family has a big ranch in eastern Oregon. This was supposed to be a supply run combined with a trip to the coast, but I have a little personal business to transact, too. I haven't been this far west in years."

16

"You know," Ashley said, then shook her head and bit her lower lip, "If I didn't know better, I'd say this was a come on just so you could hold my hand." She sat up straight and squared her shoulders. "I gotta tell you, if you're after money, I don't have any. I live with my grandmother and we're just poor folks, scrambling to make a living."

Wyatt quickly dropped her hand, shocked and hurt at the same time, his chest suddenly icy cold, as if someone had stabbed him with an icicle. "N-n-no! I, I, I w-w-wouldn't d-d-do that!"

Ashley picked up his hand, no longer warm and soft, but cold and tense. She rubbed her other hand on top of it, warming it with positive thoughts of harmony and apology. "I'm sorry," she said. "Really, I am. I've had so many people try to con me in my life. Not many guys give me a second look. Well, except for the old or scroungy-looking ones who are looking for a meal ticket. Or they're looking for drugs. I guess they figure anyone with a movement disorder is bound to have a big fat prescription for muscle relaxants."

"Yeah, there's a whole new group of Baclofen aficionados out there." Wyatt looked down at his uneaten burger, uncomfortable with the new topic of conversation. *Shut up and finish lunch!* Wyatt gently pulled his hand away. "I'd b-b-better eat," he said, wincing at the return of his stutter. He took a big bite of the juicy burger, then tapped on his smartphone to check the time. An unintentional groan escaped. Instead of the time, a calendar reminder popped up. The countdown icon showed he had ten minutes until he had to be at the escrow office to sign the final papers for purchasing the new property and horse stables.

Rather than try to explain, he crammed another bite of burger in his mouth, wrapped up the lunch he wouldn't be able to finish, then flashed the front of his smartphone at Ashley, letting her see he had an appointment in just a few minutes. He stood up, shrugged his shoulder as a silent 'I'm sorry,' then pocketed the phone. A long drink of the root beer to wash down his hasty lunch, and he was ready to go.

Sort of. He'd try it without touching her. "B-b-bye," he said, then tipped his head and reached up to mime doffing his hat. He frowned and exhaled in frustration as he turned away from her, then grabbed his uneaten food, hastily shoving it in the trash. *Why couldn't I be glib like Colton? I can't even utter a simple good-bye!*

Chapter 3
A New Old Place

Wyatt checked the garish oversized digital clock on the wall as he walked into the escrow building, a brisk two-block walk from The Dairy Barn. The one-foot tall red numbers indicated he was only one minute late. His hastily eaten burger gurgled in his gut but wasn't threatening a major upset stomach. He stifled a root beer burp as he sat down, coughing softly to disguise the noise. *Phew! Now I feel better.*

An older man dressed in a wrinkled sky blue button-down shirt with a poorly knotted red tie came out of the back office, a manila folder in his hand. "Mr. Younger?" he asked and looked right at Wyatt.

Wyatt stood up and nodded, then followed him to the back of the office. *Let's hope he's not a chatty Charlie and doesn't want anything more than signatures and initials out of me. And a check.* Wyatt tapped his chest pocket, verifying he hadn't forgotten to bring them. He still had two blank checks. *The escrow office said to make sure and bring a check, but there's always someone else wanting money when closing a deal.*

"Hi, I'm Charles Whitman, but you can call me Charlie," the balding man said as he reached out to shake Wyatt's hand.

He really is a Charlie? Wyatt blinked back his chuckle and shook the man's hand vigorously, trying to assert confidence, not dominance.

"Let's get right down to business, shall we?" Charlie asked, holding open the door into a small but private room.

Before he sat down, Wyatt picked up the straight back chair and brought it closer to Charlie's desk. He wanted to make sure he didn't drop anything when handing papers back and forth. It had been a while since purpose stress had plagued him, but he was tense. Being tense was always a gateway to his frailty. *Not today! New business, new town, new home, new friends.*

"You're getting quite a good deal on this old place," Charlie said. "The house may be over a hundred years old, but the barn and stables were put up only twenty years ago and all the major buildings have steel roofing. You couldn't buy five acres of raw land for what you're paying for these five acres with the six buildings."

Chatty Charlie wasn't telling him anything he didn't already know, so Wyatt smiled weakly, nodded, then returned to his stone-faced expression. *You and I both know that three of the buildings are worthless and I'll have to pay someone to take them down and haul the mess away. And you just said you wanted to get right down to business. I've already said I wanted it, so no sales pitch required. Let's get on with it!*

"I just need you to sign a few waivers. That old wood stove in the house has to go. It's a fire hazard and not certified. By signing these two documents you agree that you are aware of its presence and you will dispose of it properly."

Wyatt pulled a fat-bodied pen out of his pocket. The name of the vendor had worn off years ago. He had replaced the ink cartridge at least ten times, but it was still his favorite writing implement. The girth and weight of the old promotional pen was perfect for his grip plus it was his good luck charm.

He barely heard the old man as he shuffled papers in front of him, using his own sterling silver slimline pen to countersign or witness all the places required to make the transaction legal. "Now, all I need are two checks. One for the title insurance, the other for the balance due the previous owner."

Wyatt pulled out the two folded over checks and showed them to Charlie.

"Looks like you came prepared, Mr. Younger. All right," Charlie shoved the last two pages over to Wyatt, "just make them out like this and I'll make copies for you. Give it a couple of days for the checks to clear, and you're ready to move in. There are a few renters still using the stables to board horses, but they all know they'll have to be cleared out at 48 hours' notice. I'll post that clear-out notice this evening.

"The house has been deserted for a year or so, as you probably already saw at the walk through. A lot of items were left behind. Everything is yours: locks, stocks, and old metal barrels. The folks from the widow's church did the best they could, but you know how it is with volunteers: you get what you pay for." Charlie laughed at his own joke, but Wyatt only smiled. *Be polite and get the heck out of this office with your paperwork as soon as possible. This guy's in love with his own voice, and his office is positively claustrophobic!*

***

Wyatt strolled through the mid-town park, the verdant

green grass splattered with daffodils and crisscrossed with puddle-covered benches. The cool moist air blowing across his face, refreshing after sharing the closet-sized office with the onion-eating heavy smoker, reminded him that he was now free to do as he pleased.

This was his town now. The place he'd come to for gas and groceries. He had already discovered an easy short cut to the other side of the one-way street and his truck. It wouldn't take him too long to figure out the traffic patterns and where the stores were in this twenty-mile-per-hour town.

Yes, it was *his* town now. No longer would he be Colton's brother or Big Jake's son. For a while, he'd be referred to as the new guy who moved into Widow Harrison's place, but soon enough, they'd call him by his name. He wouldn't have to worry that his new friends and business contacts would see him solely as a port to plug into to get money. Western Oregon was practically a different country from where he grew up in the eastern part of the state. Chatty Charlie hadn't even blinked when he said the last name Younger. With his inheritance safe in the bank, he had enough to live on for years, even with the renovations he had planned.

He took another deep breath. Fresh air. Perfect for his

fresh start. All he needed was to make the three-hour trip back to Dad's place, spend a few hours there to finish packing and cleaning up, and then a celebration dinner with the family. He'd get up early to hit the road, then do his 'big' shopping in Salem to stock up on the essentials. His brain was ready to relocate but he still had to clear up his old life as best he could.

After the proper 48 hours' notice was given to those who were boarding their horses at his stables, he'd be in his own place. No sharing responsibilities or making excuses. Hurry up, deadline! Mine, mine, all mine!

Plus, his new hometown was magical. He had just met the most wonderful, spunky woman, an angel whose magic touch erased his stutter…

Shoot! I forgot to get her phone number!

Double shoot! I don't even know her last name!

How was he ever going to find her again, find his Ashley?

Don't panic. You know where she'll be next Tuesday. She's a student at the community college. Even though Colton was only substitute teaching there and you don't know the name of the regular teacher, you do know which classroom she'll be in and at what time. Just keep busy with setting up the new old place, and you'll be fine.

Chapter 4
Training with the Prince

"Ashley, I just saw a flyer posted down at the post office and another one just like it at Harvey's Market. It looks like we'll all have to make sure to have our horses and tack out of the stables by noon day after tomorrow. The sale finally went through on Widow Harrison's old place."

Angry, Ashley tried to toss her boot across the mud room, then became even more ticked off when it slipped from her grip and landed a measly two feet away. "But Grandma, it's finally stopped raining. I was just getting ready to start riding again," she moped.

"I'm sorry, dear. We both knew it was coming. That old place has been for sale for almost two years now. It was only out of the goodness of Sharon's heart that she let you and a few others use it for boarding and training while she was caretaker. The Prince will just have to come back up here. I know he's still skittish when it comes to climbing up the hill and dealing with road noises and dogs barking, but he'll just have to get used to life here. Otherwise, what we have is an oversized dog for you to feed and clean up after. He threw you off one too many times, as far as I'm concerned. I won't let you ride on him until he's completely broke. Maybe you ought to get something tamer to take care of, like a goat."

"You know I can't ride a goat!" Ashley blurted out in frustration. "And I don't want or need another dog. The Prince will be fine. I took my old radio down to the stables. I've been playing tapes of barking dogs and loud truck noises for two weeks now."

"Does it make a difference?" Grandma asked.

Ashley reached up to wipe her chin just as a spasm hit and she smacked herself in the mouth. *Umph!* "No, not yet," she grunted. "But it will. I know he'll get used to the sounds soon."

"Well, regardless, we need to bring him back here before tomorrow noon. It's too late to do anything about it tonight. I guess I'll have to call in to work and tell them I have an appointment." She sighed. "It's a good thing they're nice folks or they'd never put up with my crazy life."

Don't get mad, Ashley. Grandma loves you and she'd do anything in the world for you. Shoot, she already does anything and everything—just for you. One of these days, you'll be independent and then she can have a life of her own again. Or a life of her own for the first time.

As soon as Grandma was out of the room, Ashley grabbed her boot and pulled it back on. *I'll go get him tonight, so she doesn't have to miss work tomorrow. It wouldn't be so bad if she hated her job or she was paid salary and time off wasn't money out of her pocket, but she really loves working at the mill and feed store. Plus, we get a great discount on feed and straw.*

Five minutes later, Ashley had negotiated the steep driveway and only tumbled once, catching herself on the mailbox post before she fell all the way forward into a four-point sprawl. She still had twenty minutes of daylight left and another ten minutes of dusk after that. If she got The Prince tonight, Grandma could swing by the stables in the morning and pick up the rest of his tack on her way into work. She wouldn't come up short on another paycheck because of her.

Just one more ride! Or at least an attempt. If Sharon has left for the day, I'll ride him bareback. Ashley groaned as she realized that wouldn't work: she couldn't get up on him by herself without at least stirrups to give her a foot up. She'd have to lead him like a lamb.

Toot! Toot! Toot, toot, toot!

"You're walking on the wrong side of the road, idiot!" the ponytailed blonde driving the silver Prius hollered as she drove past her, the silent electric-powered vehicle startling Ashley.

And there she went again, back into another blackberry-covered ditch. Surprised by the car's sudden appearance, her slow neurological reactions caused her to tumble over her own feet, her hands not coming up in time to protect her face. As it sped past her, kicking up gravel and grit, the driver never even looked in her rearview mirror to see that she had caused an accident. Or she did look and didn't care…

***

"Oh, my God. Where did that girl go off to now?" Grandma Florine opened every door and closet in the house, then searched every stall and shed on the small one-acre property. Her knees weakened, and she clutched the back of the kitchen chair as she realized where she must be. "I'll bet that knucklehead went to bring her horse back here by herself. In the dark!"

She grabbed her big flashlight and stomped down the hill. "Ashley!" Ashley!" she called out as she shone her

29

incandescent beam in a crisscross pattern, searching for her headstrong granddaughter, at the same time, making sure she was visible to oncoming traffic.

Florine hiked the quarter mile to the stables and found it deserted. At least of people. Three horses were still in their stalls, snickering at the prospect of getting a treat from a human visitor. "Not tonight, guys," she told them, then turned back up the road to home.

Maybe she fell asleep in her room. I forgot to check her messy bed to see if she was sleeping in it. She's going to get a piece of my mind when I get back! Scaring me half to death!

Not much will give a woman more strength and adrenaline than being angry. She stomped back towards the house and was halfway there when she heard it from the gulley.

"Grandma?"

Florine turned around and shone the flashlight at the sound. "Oh, my God! Are you okay, Ashley?"

Ashely was a tangle of prickly vines and body parts, a few jutting out in the wrong direction. Her face was dark with the uneven lines of bloody scratches and still embedded thorny blackberry stringers. "Hold on, darling. I still have the pruners in my hip pocket."

Grandma set the long torch-style flashlight on the edge of the road and climbed into the ditch, pruning shears in hand. She snipped and snipped, then made sure whatever piece was stuck to Ashley was removed as gently as possible. Two days later, or so it felt like to the women, Ashley was free of her botanical bindings.

"Hold onto my arm and let me see if I can pull you out," Grandma said, then grasped her granddaughter's elbow, her mama bear strength returning despite the fatigue of a long work day. "Good God, girl! I think you broke your arm!"

"I think so, too," Ashley said softly, then gave up on trying to be strong and started crying. "I'm sorry I went by myself. I just didn't want to be a burden and cause you to miss any more work. And here I am, all messed up and The Prince is still...."

Her words were cut off by a full-blown blubbering sob fest. She brought up her unbroken arm and tried to wipe her nose and missed, smacking the semi-coagulated slash on her forehead, causing it to start weeping into her face again.

"What use am I? I'm just a burden. Why am I even alive?"

Florine held her close to her bosom. "You're here for me,

and for you, too. You'll find out what your purpose is sometime later. Maybe never. But know that you are my pride, joy, and blessing and one of the reasons I keep on living every day. So, knock off that 'Oh, woe is me' shit and let's get you out of this ditch and to the doctor. I can't see any place that you need stitches, but if that arm isn't broken, it's certainly dislocated. Either way, we have insurance and I know how to use it. And if you want to look on the bright side, I'll get paid for staying home with an injured family member. So, stop worrying about money! There's always a reason for everything, no matter how miserable it seems at the time."

Ashley pulled away and reached out her good arm to Grandma for help in getting up, then noticed her erratic jerky movements were less than normal. "Maybe I broke something in the right way."

"Or maybe having a good cry and deciding not to stress works on your involuntary movements, too." Grandma patted her hand, then helped her up out of the ditch. "Let's go to the emergency room. I'll drive through and pick up French fries and milkshakes so we have something to eat while we're waiting to be seen. No use going hungry and hurting, too."

***

"Hi. I'm Dr. Williams. And you are?"

"I'm Florine Hunter, Ashley's grandmother, and also the one who's raised her since she was three pounds."

"Well, Florine, you were right. Her shoulder was dislocated. I'm surprised she wasn't screaming. That's a very painful injury. We got her situated with ice packs and pain relievers. Because of her involuntary movements, though, I'd like to keep her here overnight for observation. She's at risk for fall, and just getting out of a car and into your house can be very stressful. Let her stay and recover in our care for a day, at least. Did she give the nurse her list of meds? We'll have to dispense them out of our pharmacy. Hospital policy, you know."

"Yeah, I know, and yes, I gave the nurse the list. I keep a copy on my phone. You must be new to this area. Sometimes I don't know if I was doing the right thing, making her learn to walk and be independent. She falls down a lot. I may have seemed tough on her when she was younger, but now she at least tries to do what every other red-blooded American girl does, including riding a horse and getting a college degree. She only uses her electric wheelchair when she's on the college campus. I hate that thing, but she's right.

She'd be flat as a flapjack if she fell down on a busy street. I'm not sure if you're aware of her condition, but her reflexes, well, they're not reflexes. She has to think about all her movements. When that blasted woman pulled right up behind her in that electric car and honked the horn, it startled her so bad, she fell. Most folks would automatically put out a hand or two to break the fall, but not my Ashley."

"You're lucky she fell in the brambles and not into the car. She may be scratched up, but she didn't tumble down a ravine, either. Go ahead and see if she's still awake and say your good nights. You need your rest, too. And you might want to start taking some vitamins, Florine."

A blush rose on Florine's dried sweat and dust-covered face. "Do I look that bad?" she asked.

"No, you look better than most women who come in with a wounded child. I just happen to know that primary care givers for special needs children, whether full-grown or not, take care of others first. She'll be independent one of these days, mark my words. She's one tough cookie."

"Yes, she is," Florine said, her chest puffed in pride.

"And so is her grandmother," the doctor said, adding a wink. "Now, if you'll excuse me, I have to go check on another patient. If all goes well, I'll release Ashley," he looked down at his watch, "in about 18 hours. Get something besides fast food to eat and remember those vitamins."

Florine giggled and shrugged her shoulders. "Yes, doctor. Will do!"

Chapter 5
Kimmie

"I came all this way and still didn't find his new place!" Kimmie bitched into her phone. "Hold on a minute, Barbie."

Kimmie put her smartphone in front of her face as she drove. "I just got this phone last week and haven't figured out the settings yet. My mom will skin me alive if I get pulled over for driving while talking on a cellphone again."

She used the pad of her finger to slide over the glass, finally finding the little gear icon. A couple more taps and she was synched to her car's Bluetooth system. "Anyhow, as I was saying, I drove all over these miserable hills out here. Not a coffee shop in sight. What in the heck is an Airlie, anyhow? Maybe it means a good place to grow Christmas trees and grapes. Not much else out here. So, anyhow, I didn't see Wyatt or his truck anywhere! I came all this way for nothing. And then some idiot was walking down the wrong side of the road. He scared the hell out of me! I thought I was going to have a heart attack."

"Kimmie, do you really think you can get Wyatt interested

in you. I mean, you were dating his brother off and on for, what? A year or was it two?"

"Three! I've been trying to get into Colton's pants since sophomore year in high school. Hey, all I had to do was let him get a little, and then say I was pregnant. It was the perfect plan to get some of that family's money. My mom said it worked for her with her first husband. A few weeks after a quick but luxurious wedding, and all I would need to do is trip and fall, and boom! 'Oh, I miscarried. We need to get a safer house, so I won't lose our next child, too.'" Kimmie laughed so hard, she had tears in her eyes.

"Yeah, well that *might* have worked, Kimmie, if he was an everyday normal Joe. Why didn't you listen to me and see the signs that Colton was gay? He was always the best dressed guy around, was the president of both the drama and glee clubs, and I don't think he ever got his hands dirty in his life. How he could do that and have a dad who was the richest rancher in the eastern half of Oregon is beyond me. Maybe he did the bookkeeping. Nah. Sorry, honey; you just picked the wrong guy."

"I just wish he wanted to at least pretend he was straight. I wouldn't care if he had boyfriends as long he gave me a beautiful house, a big fat checking account, and let me have a guy or two on the side, too."

"Too bad his folks were progressive. Or open-minded or whatever it is they're calling it these days. I hear it was a beautiful wedding. Two Ken dolls on top of a five-tier wedding cake. Of course, our families weren't invited…"

"What a waste of two nice bodies. There's sure to be at least one big pecker between the two of them," Kimmie sighed.

"Wake up and watch the road, girlfriend. Unless they decide to become exhibitionists, you'll never find out," Barbie said. "And forget about his little brother, Wyatt. You were so mean to him in high school—teasing him about his stutter—I doubt he'd bless you if you sneezed."

"Hmm, I don't know about that…" Kimmie turned to her left to make sure there wasn't an oncoming car, then headed onto the highway. "I hear that if you can get a guy to have at least two drinks with you, you can have your way with him for the rest of the night. His common sense and guard disappear by the time he's had his third drink, and by the fourth or fifth, you've convinced him to get a room. A couple more mixed drinks for him in the room—heavy on the hard liquor for him while I consume nothing but mixers—and I'm as good as engaged to a Younger. I wouldn't even have to sleep with Wyatt. I'd just strip him after he passed out drunk, slip off most or all my clothes, and be at his side when he wakes up in the morning, cooing in his ear about what a great time we had last night, how happy I was he asked me to be his bride."

"Wh-wh-why would you w-w-want to be m-m-married to that freak?" Barbie asked mockingly. "You'd be the laughing stock of all our friends. Can you imagine all of us getting together at a party? I'm sure my Jim and Elsa's husband, Jim, would make your high school teasing seem tame by comparison. Get your head out of his family's bank accounts and find someone else to sink your acrylic claws into. Even some old geezer with one foot in the grave would be better. Find one, give him one night of heaven, then pump him full of soybeans and saltpeter. Even little blue pills won't help after that regimen. He'll feel so guilty about not being able to please you, you'll wind up with more jewelry than Tiffany's. At least, that's what my mother said about her second husband, God rest his soul."

"Yeah, well, I still think a quick in and out marriage to Wyatt would be best for my bank account and reputation.

Then again, a few months of bedding someone who takes forever to get something out might mean he takes his time in bed, too."

"Ew!"

"Don't diss him too quickly, Barbie. He's easy on the eyes, seems to be a gentle sort, and then there's all that money Papa left him. I'll see if I can get chummy with his mother, find out what her interests are and haunt the same places. I mean, a woman has to have a hobby other than shopping, right?"

"Nope. Shopping is enough for me," Barbie said. "And nightclubbing to show off the new clothes, shoes, and bling."

Chapter 6
A New Life

Just concentrate on moving boxes and pulling down plywood walls and rotten rafters. Once you get this container filled, Harvey said his guy would haul it away and bring out another empty one. If what you're tearing down is too sturdy for a crowbar and sledgehammer, you can always rent an excavator to chomp it to pieces with a demolition bucket. Don't wear yourself out too much but get as much done as you can by Monday afternoon. You don't want to show up at the college on Tuesday at ten, all worn out, with dark circles under your eyes. I'll see you soon, Ashley!

Wyatt tossed the last piece of decayed flooring into the ten-yard dumpster container, then took off his filthy and worn-out leather work gloves and threw them in, too. *It's a good thing I buy them by the dozen. Looks like I need to get another dozen next time I'm in town.*

Out came the smartphone again, ready to take more pictures of his work in progress. Wyatt scrolled through the images he had taken in the past four days, then looked up and grinned. *Progress! Definite progress.* He noticed the time. *Where'd the day go? I wasn't going to work late today and it's already after five. Okay. Grab your overnight bag and get to town. No kitchen-sink bath and microwaved burritos for supper tonight. A long hot shower at the motel and a rib eye steak and baked potato dinner will help me get a good nights' sleep. That, and a climate-controlled room with a real bed instead of a camp cot!*

***

Cock-a-doodle-doo! Cock-a-doodle-doo!

Wyatt reached over and shut off the cyber rooster alarm on his smartphone, then realized his lip hurt. His mouth was dry, but his grin was so wide, it threatened to split his bottom lip.

It's a good thing I set the alarm. I must have been more tired than I thought. Ten hours of sound sleep. I don't think I even turned over. Already 8:30? Still plenty of time to clean up, grab a cup of coffee and a donut from the breakfast buffet, and check out at the front desk. Then it's time for school. Again. Ashley's class starts at ten o'clock!

Wyatt was at the college half an hour before class started, so eager he couldn't sit still. The classroom door was still locked, so he walked around the campus, staying within sight of the psychology building where his brother had been the substitute lecturer. The place where he had met the first woman in his life who didn't intimidate him. No. Wait. It wasn't the lack of intimidation with Ashley. She was self-assured and dynamic despite her halting speech and being confined to a powered wheelchair. She could terrorize anyone if she cared to, even sitting down. No, she brought out something in him, like a cable that had been buried and never discovered, a toughness and confidence he never knew he had. Yes, he wanted to help and protect her, but by her attitude, she didn't *need* anyone. He'd known for years that he didn't *need* anyone, either.

Not needing was not the same as not wanting.

And he definitely wanted her.

Yes, he didn't stutter when he touched her, but that wasn't a reason to search her out or to make her part of his life. It wasn't the *reason*, but it was an *indication*, like a sign from above. Whether that sign was cosmic or Divine, he didn't care. He just wanted to find her. Again. This time, he'd make sure he got her phone number and email address. Who knew? Maybe if the cosmos or whatever decided they were right for each other, she'd want to share his new home with him. And maybe his life…

Wyatt reached up and wiped his mouth with the back of his hand, hopefully erasing the insanely-happy idiot grin he knew he sported. He glanced at his watch, verifying the time. He watched the classroom door from a nearby picnic table as men and women straggled in, their numbers increasing as the time neared ten o'clock.

Had he missed seeing her go in the room? No way! But he'd amble over and pretend he belonged in the classroom to make sure she wasn't there.

He passed through the portals of learning, the walls covered in the stereotypical posters of inspiration he'd seen since he was in middle school. Nope. She wasn't here. Yet. No one seemed to notice that he wasn't a registered student, so he pulled up a folding chair in the back of the room and got as comfortable as he could. Or at least, he tried to look that way. He leaned back, crossed one ankle over his knee and pulled out his smartphone, checking his numbers again, pretending that he was getting ready to take notes.

Just like every other time he'd checked his monitor, all his sine waves, volts and amps were spot on. His deep brain stimulators had been tuned to perfection six months ago, his spastic movements completely under control. Dr. Downs had said that he'd never seen anyone take so well to the procedure. His new-style batteries should last at least four years, maybe longer. As long as he didn't get an MRI and made sure he showed the TSA guys at the airport his little 'medical device implant' card, no one would ever know. The tell-tale scars where horns should be growing out of his head and the hairline scars behind his ears were grown over with his thick dark curls. The sub-clavicle scars where his generators were implanted could have been where he'd scraped himself falling out of a tree or tumbling off a bike. He wasn't a bear as far as chest hair, but someone would have to be up close and personal to be able to see those scars, too.

Up close and personal? Dang! Where is that girl!

Wyatt sat in on the class, only the adrenaline of anxiety keeping him awake during the boring lecture on leadership development in new markets. *No wonder the students last week were in awe of Colton's presentation. This guy could make a mint if he could bottle his nod-off persona and sell it to insomniacs!*

Finally, the teacher finished his lecture and dismissed the class. One student remained at his desk, fast asleep, the long-haired young man's head tipped back into a position that made him look like a pelican swallowing a fish. Wyatt got up from his seat in the back of the room and walked past him, gently nudging him awake on his way to the front of the class and the teacher.

Gasp! Sputter!

Wyatt looked over his shoulder at the napper and winked. *I'm sure you'd do the same for me, buddy.*

"Thanks," Sleepy whispered, then gathered his notes and hustled out of the classroom.

"I was looking for Ashley," Wyatt said to the teacher, foregoing any introductions that would give him even more opportunities to stutter. "Sh-she was here last week when my b-brother taught your class."

"So, you're Colton's brother?" the professor asked.

Wyatt nodded, then waited. It was obvious the teacher was fishing.

"I heard lots of good reports on his lecture," the professor said, then waited for Wyatt to speak again.

Wyatt nodded once more. He wasn't certain, but just the

thought of what the man was probably thinking hurt. *Yes, yes. It's hard to live up to someone as dynamic as my brother, especially since he's so handsome and well-spoken, and I have a stutter.*

The professor thought twice about commenting on how articulate his brother was, then decided he'd at least address the man's concern.

"I didn't see Ashley here today. She's usually as dependable as winter rain in Oregon."

"Her last n-n-name?"

The professor shook his head and grimaced. "Sorry, son, but if she didn't give it to you, I can't." He looked over at the crowd of students, hovering over their smartphones. "Why don't you ask one of them. They didn't have to sign any confidentiality agreements."

Wyatt sighed in resignation, then gave the sixty-ish professor a thumbs-up as thanks.

"You're welcome, son," he said. "She's a tough cookie. And smart, too. I'm sure you'll find her if it was meant to be."

A dark cloud of anger changed Wyatt's smile to a clenched-jaw scowl.

"It's a small town and she's easy to describe," the

embarrassed teacher said. "As I said, I'd tell you if I could. Ask around. Someone's sure to know more about her."

Wyatt's demeanor softened, and he shrugged with an attitude of truce. He turned to leave, then looked back and gave a casual flick of the wrist good-bye wave. *Thanks for nothing. Or maybe I should say, 'Thanks for not being a jerk and telling me to buzz off.'*

And there he was, Mr. Sleepy Student. *Man up and ask him!*

Wyatt tapped the now alert twenty-something student on the shoulder. "Excuse me, b-b-but do you know where Ashley is today?"

"You mean the gal in the souped-up wheelchair?"

Wyatt winked and pointed his index finger at him. *You betcha, pardner!*

"I didn't see her today. She's usually here. If she's around, she's pretty easy to spot with that hot rod scooter of hers."

"Do you have her n-n-number or know her last n-n-name?"

"Sorry, but I don't. She pretty much keeps to herself. I mean, she pops up and gives the professors hell all the time, as in holds them to task and all. But I don't know anyone here who sees her socially. Sorry."

Just as Mr. Sleepy Student turned away, he spun back around. "Hey, wait! I just remembered something. A couple times she mentioned stuff about riding. I mean, horses. I don't think she lives in town but comes in on one of the community shuttles. If she owns a horse, and I kinda got the impressions she does, then she probably lives out of town."

"Cool! Thanks!" Wyatt said, and gave him a fist-bump.

Maybe she missed the shuttle. Or maybe she had a cold, but either way, she'll probably be here next week. Countdown!

***

Wyatt kept busy with his renovations. Now that the small outside canning kitchen and tacky woodshed were demolished, he had a clean slate to start with. The last bits of debris were hauled away and he'd leveled the driveway with his little orange Kubota tractor, at least good enough for him. Now it was time to finish drawing the designs for the new structures. He squirmed as he tried to get comfortable in the plastic folding chair at the banquet table that served as a kitchen table and drafting desk. He glanced over at the rolled flooring at the far end of the living room, just waiting for him to have some extra time to lay it out. *Not yet. The barn and stables have to be finished before the mustangs are rounded up. My comfort can come later.*

The existing barn structures needed work. He felt a bit guilty about not allowing the horses that had been stabled here to stay, but it was easier to leave all the gates open during the day when he was clearing out the various degrees of aging stable muck. He piled all of it at the far end of the property into two piles. He wasn't much of a farmer but did know that he was supposed to alternate layers of animal waste with green clippings. He'd only mowed the lawn once and already spread out the first layering of cut grass, topping it with the most rotted manure. By the end of the summer, he'd have the best compost available. He didn't have the time or energy to put in a kitchen garden this year, but it would definitely be a priority for next spring.

The days went by quickly. As he went in Harvey's Market to pick up a half gallon of milk and a few bananas for his morning cereal, Wyatt decided to pick up a newspaper. He hadn't read one in ages and there might be something he needed to know. The second thing he noticed, after the headlines, was the date. "Is it T-t-tuesday already?" he asked the clerk.

"Yup, it sure is. Time flies when you're working hard. Anything else for you this morning, Wyatt?"

Wyatt groaned softly, then looked at his watch and shook his head. It was already nine o'clock. He barely had time to change out of the work clothes he'd worn for two days, much less shower and shave. He shoved a five-dollar bill onto the counter. "No, I'm g-g-good, Kathy," he said and left, trying to figure out whether a baby wipes sponge bath and quick change of clothes would be enough. *It's going to have to be. As it is, I'll barely make it to class dismissal time.*

He arrived ten minutes before class was over. Rather than try and sneak into the classroom, he waited at the picnic bench just outside the room. If she had come to class today, he'd see her leave through the only exit soon enough. *Calm your breathing, dude.*

Wyatt chewed his knuckle as he watched the students leave the classroom. The second to the last one out was Sleepy, followed by a frowning professor. *He probably fell asleep during the lecture again. Go ahead and talk to him. Maybe she left early…*

"Hi, there," Wyatt said.

"Oh, hey," Sleepyman said. "You didn't miss much today."

He rubbed his eyes, then amended his remark. "I don't think you missed much, but once again, I slept through the whole class. I feel bad, and I really do try to stay awake, but I work an overnight shift. I get off work, grab something for breakfast, and then bam! You'd think I'd polished off a turkey dinner the way I conk out."

Wyatt smiled, then waited to see if there was more to the story.

"I'll bet you're looking for Ashley again, huh?"

Wyatt nodded, and said, "Yes, I am. I'm n-n-not a stalker or anything…"

"Dude, you're looking for a woman who obviously didn't give you her phone number. Do you even know her last name?"

Wyatt shook his head and tried not to grimace, but it didn't work.

Sleepy laughed at him. "Yup, you're a stalker, all right. Nah, you're not out to hurt her, I'm sure. I'll save you some trouble, though. Next week is spring break. She's not gonna be here. Well, she might come, but the other students and the teachers won't be here. Why don't you give me your number? If I happen to see her, I'll give it to her. That way, she can make the decision on whether to call you or not just in case you are some sort of pervert."

"I'm not a p-p-pervert!" Wyatt exclaimed. "We had l-l-lunch together. I had an appointment and f-f-forgot to get her n-n-number before I left!"

"Ew. Don't you hate it when that happens..." Sleepy said, then laughed.

"Yes, I do. V-v-very much." Wyatt scribbled his name on the back of the receipt for the paper from Harvey's and handed it to him.

"Sorry. I'll see what I can do. Oh, I'm Caleb, by the way, but you can call me Cupid." Caleb glanced at the name and number, then toasted with an invisible mug. "Here's to finding the right woman, Wyatt, whether it's Ashley or not!"

Wyatt reached up and returned the mimed toast, "Here, here!" he shouted.

Hope, hope!

Chapter 7
Florine

Wyatt immersed himself in the renovation of the hundred-year-old semi-rural site at the edge of the little twenty-mile-an-hour town, trying to bury his frustration of not being able to re-connect with the most intriguing woman he'd ever met. Western Oregon days usually started with several hours of cool, penetrating fog, so he spent that time under cover, measuring and cutting wood, nailing together subassemblies so building walls would be fast and easy. By nine o'clock, sunshine and clouds were playing tag, sunshine usually winning the duel, but not before a few dark clouds spat out not-much-more-than-a-spritz of moisture for a few minutes.

Enjoy the wet while you can. We may not need it now but when June gets here, rain will be rare. Stock tanks are clean and full. Being connected to city water is a blessing, but I'll make use of the God-given gifts while they're available, especially free irrigation for the pasture, deep watering for the fruit trees and grape vines.

"Hey, there!" an older woman in mud boots called out.

Wyatt walked over to the steel corral fence and pulled it open, letting the short and sassy gray-haired woman in a scissors-modified OSU sweatshirt onto the property.

"So, you're the guy who bought this old fixer-upper. I'm glad to see someone young came in and turned it around. There was a lot of work to be done, but it looks like you've made great headway in the last few weeks. Hi, I'm Florine Hunter. I live up the road a bit. You've probably never come my way, though, since the road only leads to a few more homes and then nothing but logging roads. My granddaughter used to board and train her horse here before you bought the place. Her horse is young and a bit skittish when it comes to cars and dogs. Plus, she's what folks nowadays call special needs. I kinda liked it when they called people like her handi-capable, but that went out of favor in a hurry."

"Wyatt Younger," he said, and pulled off his glove to shake her hand.

Ashley's grandmother looked at her hand, still dirty from doing chores, and wiped it on her back pocket. "You'd have been better off leaving on the gloves," she said and chuckled. "Anyhow, I noticed you have the stalls all set up and the fences mended. That electric fence will work a lot better than those old shipping pallets Sharon piled up along the posts. She used them to fill in the gaps in the old barbed wire fence that'd been up since Moses wore braces. They worked but they were sure ugly."

They both chuckled, but Wyatt knew what she wanted: a place for her granddaughter's horse.

"Yes, you know what I'm going to ask," Florine said sheepishly. "It would mean a lot if she could come down here and at least walk The Prince around here in the arena. Her horse definitely needs more training, but he's not what's important now. Working with him is good exercise for her balance. She loses her concentration and strength over the winter by sitting around the house most of the day. When she walks him, holding onto his reins, it gives her confidence and focus. When she was a year old, the doctors told me she'd be confined to a wheelchair for the rest of her life, but I wouldn't listen to them. I made her exercise and tried my best to get her to walk by herself. Shoot, I couldn't even get her to walk around furniture until she was three years old! When she was old enough to understand, I told her that yes, part of her brain was broke, but there were plenty of other parts that worked just fine. We'd train those parts to take over the walking, talking, and balance areas that were damaged. I set up a gym in our living room for us. I try to get her to use it every day but hey, coming outside and spending time with The Prince is much more appealing."

Florine lifted up the bucket she had brought with her. "Well, I don't have time to use the gym much because I do most of the chores, but I'm a tough coach." As she set the empty pail down, she saw the start of a negative response on Wyatt's face.

"Oh, and don't worry about a little kid coming over to bug you about working her horse. Ashley's a full-grown woman."

Before he sputtered out his response, Wyatt took a deep breath to compose himself and asked, "Ashley?"

"Yes, that's her name... Oh, do you go to the college, too? You might have seen her around, scooting all over the place in her little modified red power wheelchair. I hate that thing."

Wyatt couldn't contain his smile then realized he probably looked perverse, a suddenly overzealous idiot. He reached up and swiped his hand across his mouth and rubbed under his nose, trying to force his face into composure, but just as soon as he thought he had accomplished restraint, the smile bounced back.

Florine shook her head when she saw his shock and joy at hearing Ashley's name and description. "So, there really is a Wyatt! I thought she hit her head and scrambled her brains when she fell, that you were an imaginary Prince Charming."

"I'm no p-p-prince," Wyatt said, then fought unsuccessfully to keep a blush from rising.

"You must be the one she's been talking about non-stop for the last month! Shoot! I shouldn't have said that. You two met at the Dairy Barn, right?"

Wyatt bit his bottom lip, sucking down his smile of embarrassment, and nodded. *This is too good to be true! Did you hit your head and you're the one dreaming now? Stop gawking and nodding like an idiot!*

"Is she home n-n-now?"

"Yes, she is. She's doing her workout routine. She's been at it two, sometimes three times a day. She has so much pent up energy lately. She had an accident and messed up her arm but is determined to come out of it better than ever."

Florine saw Wyatt's frown of concern and addressed it. "Ashley almost got hit by some mouthy, bitchy blonde speeding down the road in one of those fancy electric cars

58

that you can't hear until they're right on top of you. She tripped and tumbled into the ditch when the woman yelled at her. She dislocated her shoulder and got scraped up a bit, but she's fine now. The worst part about it was she had to miss her classes. Since part of her recovery was during spring break, she's only three weeks behind and should be able to catch up. The good thing, though, is she became more diligent in her exercise routine. She was getting lazy... Oh, shoot. That's too much personal information. Well, would you like to come up to the house and see her? You can stay for dinner, too. I've got a macaroni and cheese casserole in the oven and a bag of salad. Dinner can be ready in five minutes. It's quick and simple but sure to fill the hole in your gut."

"That would be g-g-great. Let me go wash up and I'll be right b-b-back."

Florine turned her bucket upside down and sat on it, elbows on her knees. "Take your time. This grandma isn't going anywhere until you get back. I don't want you to get lost. Again."

***

The driveway up to Florine and Ashley's house was not

only sinuous, but steep. "Now you can see why it's so important that Ashley keeps her balance when she walks," Florine said as she led the way up the switchback-style gravel path. "There's no way she could get up this in an electric wheelchair. As it is, I have to put my Jeep in four-wheel drive to get to the house in the winter. This driveway was almost a deal breaker on the sale, but it was such a low price for so much property, I had to take it. I put this place in a trust, so after I'm gone, at least Ashley will have a home."

Unless she finds a husband and moves in with him. Whoa, Wyatt! What's got into you? You're obsessing. She's not your first girlfriend, but you'd better be careful because you're probably the first guy who's shown an interest in her. You're just looking for a friend. She might not be the type of person you hope she is, either.

Florine showed Wyatt into the front room, the former sunken living room all laid out with a weight bench, rowing machine, and a treadmill. Since the only chair was a recliner, piled high with folded laundry, he sat on the end of the weight bench. "Would you like some iced tea?" his hostess asked.

"Yes, p-p-please," Wyatt answered then looked around at the framed photos on the walls.

"Yes, that's my Ashley," Florine said, handing him a cold bottle of iced tea. "She was a cutie. Oh, pardon the, well, the mess." She thumped on the vintage all-in-one free-weight machine with the duct taped seat and leg-lift pegs. "We don't get many visitors. No. Scratch that. We don't get any visitors. Functional space is more important."

Wyatt ignored her apology but addressed the other subject. "She's still a cutie," he said, then turned away from her and blushed. *Why did you say that!*

"Yes, I think she's still a cutie. I heard the shower running when we came in. I'll go make sure..."

"Grandma, we're out of conditioner," Ashley called out as she walked into the room, swallowed up in an oversized Oregon Beavers tee shirt, her hair wrapped in a towel.

"I bought more last week. It's in the hall closet. By the way, I think I've arranged it so you'll be able to take The Prince back to the stables for training again. I went down there earlier today and met the new owner."

Wyatt remained still on the weight bench, biting his knuckle to hide the grin on his face. Florine looked over at him and winked, trying to keep nonchalance in her voice, while Ashley looked through the refrigerator for something to drink.

"Do we have any more tea?" Ashley asked. "And is dinner almost ready? I'm starved. I added five more reps to my routine today."

"I'm sorry, but I just gave the last tea to our guest, but I can mix up some orange juice."

"Nah, I'll drink water. No, wait." Ashley shut the refrigerator door and stared at her grandmother. "Guest? Where?" She touched the towel on her head and turned around. "Why didn't you tell…"

Wyatt and Florine both rushed as Ashley tumbled forward, the shock of seeing Grandma's guest causing her to lose her balance.

"Wyatt?"

"That's what he said his name was. Is this the same Wyatt from the college?" Florine asked.

Ashley's face bloomed scarlet as she realized that now Wyatt knew she had been talking to her grandmother about him.

Wyatt ignored the tension and reached out to push the towel back in place on her head. "Are you okay?"

"Yes, I'm just clumsy. How'd you get here?"

"I walked."

"From where?" Ashley asked, then looked over at her grandma and scowled.

Wyatt pulled his hand back to his side. "J-j-just up the road," he said, tipping his head in that direction.

"So, you're the one who bought the stables? What are you going to use them for? Why didn't you let folks keep their horses there? Where have you been for these last weeks and why..." Ashley snorted in disgust, mad that her original anger about losing a place to train her horse had suddenly turned to personal frustration on why he hadn't called her. *Shoot! You only talked to him once, girl!*

Wyatt pulled out the copy of the newspaper article that had started him on his personal quest, the story about the Bureau of Land Management capturing some of the younger and prettier wild mustangs in eastern Oregon and relocating them to stables where horse-loving volunteers would break the horses, or at least get them to the point where they could be handed off or sold to interested parties. The grasslands were verdant, but the horses were reproducing so quickly, the areas were in danger of being overgrazed.

Florine came to Ashley's side and held the paper still so

they could both read it. "So, you're one of those people working to save America's wild horses?"

Wyatt nodded and grinned. "And get them n-n-new homes with folks who wouldn't b-b-be able to afford one otherwise."

Ashley moved close to him and set her hand on his arm. "Like therapy horses for handicapped kids?" *Will this still work?*

"Kids, adults, at-risk teenagers, recovering addicts, folks with PTSD..." Wyatt took a deep breath, an unintentional smile rising. *Her touch still stops my stutter! Plus, it feels good to be so close to her.*

Wyatt cleared his throat of leftover emotion and continued. "I can do the heavy lifting and repairs for the stables, fences, and hauling in hay, and I've made a few friends while researching the adoption process. My friend and I can break the horses, but I need an admin assistant to deal with, well, everything else. I'm not very good at writing letters or press releases, filling out forms or answering phone calls. Do you think you'd like to help me promote a good cause?"

"Can I at least comb out my hair and change clothes first?" Ashley answered, then they all laughed. "Yes, I think I've had enough of school for a while. I don't think a degree will make a difference when taking down names and phone numbers. Oh, and I already know how to write press releases and grant proposals. When do we start?"

Florine removed Ashley's hand from Wyatt's arm and frowned. "You're not starting until after dinner, at the earliest. And don't go getting all handsy, granddaughter. You just met this man and he's still your boss."

Ashley looked at Wyatt and winked.

As soon as Florine's attention was on taking the casserole out of the oven, Wyatt winked back. *Thanks for not telling her that your touch stopped my stutter. I don't think she'd understand.*

Chapter 8
Kimmie the Sleuth

"And there she is," Kimmie announced to herself, her mischievous smile wide, her chemically-whitened and mechanically-straightened teeth betraying the ugly person hiding within.

Kimmie's stalking had paid off. Wyatt's mother was walking down the long driveway, a package held close to her chest, her target: the mailbox at the end of the driveway. "You may be the only Mrs. Younger now, but you won't be the last Mrs. Younger to reside at this estate. Give me a year or two, and you'll be long gone. Whether it's battling bitches in prison or diddling boy toys in Majorca is your decision. Play nice with me and we can share the Younger family fortune. Try and keep me at bay and you'll find out what a woman scorned is all about."

To Kimmie, having everything she wanted was all that mattered. As her stepdaddy used to say, never make little Kimmie or her mother angry. He found out the hard way how true it was.

"Yeah, well, he'll be eligible for parole in another five years or so." She batted her eyelashes and sniffed, replaying her greatest performance. "But your honor, I didn't ask for him to touch me. And he only did it when we were alone. He said something about witnesses or something like that..." *Sniff, sniff.*

"That sure taught him not to deny me what I wanted! Just because I wasn't old enough to drive yet didn't mean I shouldn't own my own Mustang! That'66 was just like the one in The Princess Diaries only a prettier blue. Who cares if it wasn't for sale or that I would have to wait three years to drive it? Daddy Bigbucks could have afforded it. Too bad all the money he had in his trust fund wasn't enough to buy him a lawyer who was more persuasive than a pissed-off thirteen-year-old!"

Kimmie watched as her prey came into view, then pulled up to the end of the long driveway leading to the Younger's estate. She stopped next to the carved timber pedestal that held the oversized mailbox. "Good morning, Mrs. Younger. Sure is a beautiful day, isn't it?"

"Oh, my!" Kate Younger said, clutching the package she had nearly dropped. "Land sakes alive, girl! That car's so quiet, I didn't even hear you drive up! You might want to put bells on it or something, so folks will know when you're coming up on 'em."

"Now, where's the fun in that?" Kimmie remarked, laughing as she recalled a few of the people she had startled since the first day she got her shiny silver Prius four months ago. When she saw real concern in Mrs. Younger's scowl, she amended her flip remark. "Bells on it? I wouldn't want folks to think a cat was sneaking up on them. I'm sure the electric car manufacturers will think of something. In the meantime, I guess I'll just keep my satellite radio turned up. A little bit of jazz should be warning enough."

Kate's initial shock had abated, and now mild disgust had taken its place. She was driving a different car and her hairstyle had changed, but this snippy blonde was still the same vicious brat who had caused Wyatt so much grief in school, all the way from kindergarten to high school, mercilessly teasing and mocking his stutter. Rumor was that her lies had sent her stepfather to prison. *I wonder what she wants now? And from me? Whatever it is, it can't be good.*

"Oh, were you going to mail a package to Wyatt?" Kimmie asked, getting out of her car to get a closer look. She inched closer to Kate, her neck craned to look at the label, trying to read the rest of the address. *The letter W! It has to be for Wyatt.* "I can take it to the post office for you."

"Oh, no need to bother. This mailbox is plenty big enough for even a large parcel. Our carrier will be around soon." Kate shoved the package in the mailbox, then slammed the cover shut, making a physical statement that she didn't want any further discussion on the subject.

That bitch! She'll find out soon enough that you don't mess around with Kimmie! What Kimmie wants, Kimmie gets!

"Oh, it's no problem at all." Kimmie tugged at the latch to open the mailbox and snapped back an acrylic nail. "Damn it!" She quickly stuck her middle finger in her mouth, panting quickly to swallow the rest of the curse words trying to shoot out.

Kate took the pause and Kimmie's partial retreat as an opening to retrieve the box. "On second thought, I think I'll drive into the post office in town. It's such a beautiful day and an iced coffee sounds good. I hope you didn't break a nail." *Serves you right, if you did. Pushy broad!*

Kate pasted on the fake smile she usually reserved for drunken business customers at the annual Christmas party, then turned away, looking back over her shoulder. "Have a nice day!" *But have it in someone else's neck of the woods. And keep away from my sons!*

Reaching for the car door latch, Kimmie smacked the same finger, this time breaking the nail off at the quick. "Son of a bitchin', mother… ergh!" When she finally got behind the wheel, she turned up the radio, certain that Mrs. Younger would hear the brassy jazz tune from where she was.

Ding! Ding! Ding!

"Damned seatbelt alarm!" Kimmie turned up the speakers louder still, drowning out the safety warning that the seatbelt wasn't fastened, then put the car in drive and sped away. "I'll get you, and your flawed sons, too," she hissed.

A hundred yards ahead, a deer ran in front of her car. She slammed on her brakes and smacked her forehead on the mirrored visor. "Well, I'll get at least one of her sons, take what I need, then toss him aside," she said, then grabbed the seatbelt and put it across her hips. "But it would be fun to take you and then both of those pretty boys out at the same time. I've never accomplished a family trifecta before. Then again, I'm still young. I may beat Mom's record yet."

***

Driving into town to get her manicure repaired, Kimmie realized that Jake, the local wannabe Lothario, worked at the post office. She glanced at the clock on the dash. The post office was still open. A little shimmy and deception should be enough for that Casanova with the bloated ego. If he thought he was going to get somewhere with her, he'd tell her anything and everything she needed to know.

Kimmie strolled into the post office lobby, head held high, lips slightly parted, and flipped her hair off her shoulder. Then she looked around. The place was empty. *That was a waste of a first-class entrance. The jerk's probably in back. Oh, but wait! That gives me better idea, one that won't take as much work. There they are: the flat rate boxes.*

She quickly pulled the tape off the ends of the box and put it together, wrote Wyatt Younger on the front, 12345 below it, and then Oregon beneath that. In the upper left where the return address went, she wrote Kimmie - Oregon. *There, that ought to do it.*

Kimmie walked up to the front counter, certain of success. *Ding! Ding! Ding!*

She smacked the classic bell sitting next to the taped, torn, and re-taped piece of cardstock with 'ring bell for service' written in faded blue ink. Just as she was getting ready to pummel the shiny chrome dome again, Jake appeared, wiping donut sprinkles from his chin.

"Oh, hi there, Kimmie. How's it going today?" he asked, then quickly wiped his sticky fingers on his belly before running them through his scented-oiled hair, sprucing up his appearance as best he could on such short notice.

"Well, it could be better." She flashed the broken fingernail on her middle finger at him and pouted, hoping for a little sympathy and maybe to arouse his inner knight-in-shining-armor persona. "Could you help me with something?"

"Absolutely. What can I do you for, I mean, what can I do for you?"

"I don't know what's got into me, Jake. I was putting this package together for Wyatt—you know, the younger Younger son—and my mind went blank. What's his zip code now?"

Jake grabbed the laminated sheet from the side of the vintage cash register. "That would be 97361. Here, do you need a pen?" He pulled one of three 'Property of US Government' pens from his pocket protector and handed it to her.

"Why, thank you." She hurriedly scribbled the zip code on

the palm of her hand, then gave him his pen back.

"Don't you want to write it on the box, too?" Jake asked.

"Oh, yes. Silly me."

"Um, Kimmie," Jake said warily, "I think you forgot the rest of his address—you don't have a street name on there, either. I mean, the postal service can deliver a package without the city written on the box as long as it has the zip code, but just writing 12345 isn't gonna cut it."

"Oh, that's the other thing. I forgot how to spell the name of that road he lives on now."

"M-A-I-N," Jake said, then turned away and rolled his eyes. *And I thought she was a bottle blonde. She's either that dense or… Crap! I just gave out an address! She's been phishing! At least the first part of the street address was probably phony. 12345. How lame.*

Jake faked a cough, then turned back to face Kimmie. "Sorry about that. I had something stuck in my throat." He reached for the box. "If this is ready to go, would you like to pay with cash or credit card?"

Kimmie snatched the box back, then flashed another phony smile. "I think I'll take it back home and toss in some of my homemade chocolate chip cookies. Wyatt loves my baking…" she cooed, then licked her lips. *A little tongue on lip action gets them hot, bothered, and amenable every time.*

"Sure thing," he said and winked. "Hope your afternoon gets better," he said, then wiggled his middle finger at her, indicating her broken fingernail, but also flipping off the phony female at the same time.

"Yeah, sure," she said dryly, then turned away and smacked the door with opened hand. She was done with the jerk and no longer needed to be sweet or personable.

"Grrr!" Jake couldn't contain his guttural growl but did hold his tongue. *Bitch! You think you're so cute, but you're as phony as your fancy fingernails, as transparent as the top coat of nail polish. I just hope your time is coming soon. Oh, and have fun on your search for your rich little wannabe boyfriend. Wyatt's new hometown of Pedee shares a zip code with the little big town of Monmouth. You'll never find him in that rambling college community, much less know that he's tucked back in the winding hills twenty miles away. Even if you did manage to find him, he'd never fall for your wiles!*

"Let's see… Okay, Google, show me the quickest route to zip code 97361."

Kimmie looked at the image on her smartphone and saw it

74

was pretty much a straight route. At least, she wouldn't have to take any exits from state route 22. "Four hours from here? Maybe I'll wait and get a fresh start tomorrow." She swiped the screen, then set the phone down in her cup holder. "Time for a latte and a fresh manicure…and maybe a new outfit." She flipped her visor down and looked in the mirror. "I don't want to show up looking like one of the locals now, do I," then cackled her evil witchy laugh. "He'll never know what hit him."

***

Dinner was done and the excited conversation about what could be done about the plight of wild horses in Oregon and what the Bureau of Land Management had proposed for them had slowed down.

"I'll clear the table and you two can finish your little business plan," Florine said, leaving the two of them alone for the first time since they had reconnected.

Wyatt brought out his smartphone, then casually moved his knee under the table toward Ashley. At first, she was startled at his touch, then realized Wyatt wasn't making a pass, but simply grounding himself.

"Here's one of the websites," he said, showing the screen to her. "Saving the mustangs is a grassroots movement, really. People who love horses are just stepping in, rounding up some of the more unique looking and better tempered young horses, and bringing them into corralled areas. After fixing any health issues and working with them for a while, they're able to decide which ones can be adopted out and which ones will go to maintained open pastures for the rest of their lives."

Ashley shook her head in amazement, but Wyatt misunderstood the gesture.

"What's wrong? I think it's a great idea. I'll be setting up one more outlet for adopting the wild horses, plus my idea is to bring in older kids and teach them responsibility by caring for and training them. Mustangs will be saved, and young people will learn to be more conscientious adults in the process."

Ashley continued to shake her head, but added a bright, sunny smile. "You do know that this is going to cost money, right? Some seriously big money."

"Yeah. So? What good is having money if you can't help others?"

Florine dropped her dish towel on the kitchen counter and came back to the table and sat across from Wyatt. "What did you say? I mean, I heard every word, but are you serious about doing this out of the goodness of your heart? How are you going to finance this—with grants you want Ashley to write or did you find Aladdin's Lamp?"

"No, no lamp. Just the goodness of my heart and a bit of money from an inheritance left to me by my father."

"Wow! Generous, good-looking, and rich, too?" Florine said. "Ashley, you be careful with this one. He's going to have the ladies crawling all over him. You might want to add bodyguard to your job description."

Wyatt shut his eyes in embarrassment and moved his leg away from Ashley. *Calm down, dude! Grandma was just making a joke!*

"It's g-g-getting late. I'd b-b-better go home."

Ashley moved her leg next to Wyatt's and meant to tap it, but an involuntary spasm caused her to smack him roughly. She swallowed hard, wanting to apologize but didn't want Grandma to know she was playing her version of footsie under the table with Wyatt. "What time do you want me to be at work tomorrow, Boss?" she asked brightly.

Wyatt looked down at his watch and chuckled. *What a great way to say I'm sorry for Grandma's remarks!* "Any time after the sun comes up but before noon. Let's say somewhere between eight and ten. It's still a little chilly and damp in the morning. We'll start earlier and work later when summer gets here."

Ashley scooted her chair back and arose awkwardly. "Yes, sir!" she said, and gave a clumsy salute. "And don't worry. I can do more than answer phones and scribble messages. I'm not afraid of dirty work, and horse poop and I have been acquainted for years. I know what it is and where to shovel it!"

"Well, that's g-g-good to know. There isn't any left to shovel now b-b-but, Lord willing, we'll have plenty by mid-summer."

Chapter 9
Tucker

"Who are you and where's Wyatt?" Ashley asked, trying to hide her disappointment at not finding her new boss and heartthrob at her old stomping grounds.

The short, barrel-chested teenager straightened up, pulled back his broad shoulders, smoothed out the wrinkles in his tee shirt, then pasted on the most courteous smile he could muster. "Good morning, ma'am. Wyatt's gone to the hardware store for some wire ties but should be back directly. He said our new secretary would be by soon. Would you be Ashley then?" he asked, certain that she was.

"Yes, I'm Ashley. And that's administrative assistant, not secretary. Who are you?"

"I'm Tucker, ma'am. I'm here to help Wyatt break the horses."

"Well, Tucker, my grandmother is a ma'am. I'm still a miss," Ashley said, and flicked her ponytail with an exaggerated twist of her neck.

Tucker couldn't help but chuckle softly. Ashley she

realized what a priss she was being and joined in, too. "I'm sorry, Tucker. I'm just a little nervous. This is my first job. At least, my first real job. I've helped out at church and volunteered on the parks and recreation committee as the secretary, but I've never had a job where I actually had to talk to customers and order supplies and stuff."

"It's my first job real job, too. I've either been in school, hanging out, getting in trouble or spending time at one of those 'retreats' that are really just juvey centers with fancy names. I did some extra stupid stuff last winter. After seeing where the guys who were eighteen wound up, I decided to get back on the straight and narrow. I'd rather be broke—couch surfing and shoveling horse sh... stuff—than incarcerated like my old buddies, living on weevil-laced rice and freezer-burnt veggies and not being able to shower alone." Tucker shuddered at the idea. "Wyatt's a cool guy. I know him 'cause our dads went to school together thirty years ago."

"They're still friends after all this time?"

"Well, they were until Wyatt's dad died. Wyatt and I weren't friends growing up, though, because he's ten years older than me. A couple years ago, he kinda adopted me as a kid brother, I guess. Adopted, took under his wing or whatever you want to call it, I'm just glad he did. He knew I loved horses as much as he did and pretty soon, I'll be working with them all day long!"

"And then be around them at n-n-night as the watchman." Wyatt stepped out of the big red Dodge dually pickup truck and handed Tucker a paper bag. "Here're the t-t-ties. Make sure the wires d-d-don't dangle into the stalls or walkways."

Wyatt doffed his hat and said, "Morning, Ashley. L-l-looks like you met T-t-tucker."

"So, he's the man who's going to help you break the horses, or at least get them calm enough to be adopted out to their new owners?"

Wyatt gave a quick nod, then motioned with his thumb for her to follow him.

He led the way into the stable, its interior renovated, but still weathered shiplap siding on the outside.

"Wow! You can't see all the changes you made from the road. This place looks brand new in here." Ashley held onto the metal gates as she walked past the stalls, her gait still unsteady but excited. "I love the smell of fresh straw. All that's missing are the horses. When are you getting them?"

Wyatt walked up to her and put his hand on the same railing, his elbow touching hers. "Tucker and I are going down to Hines tomorrow or the next day. There's really not much to do right now, but I wanted to give you the opportunity to look around. If you'd like, Tucker and I can go up to your place and bring The Prince down here."

"Oh, I don't know if he'll let you. He's pretty snobby," Ashley said, then laughed. "He thinks I'm his princess and everyone else is a peon."

Wyatt pulled his elbow in, away from her. It felt good, but Florine was right. If he was going to have a boss/employee relationship with her, he'd have to back away from the feelings that he had been holding on to for the last month. If she was the right one for him, she'd still be around six months down the road. For now, he really did need someone dependable to help coordinate interviews between the new prospective owners and the horses. It wasn't going to be easy, but if she was as passionate about all horses as she was her own, she'd bear the emotional weight of the work while he and Tucker did the heavy lifting and training.

"Got it all done, Boss," Tucker said. "Did you have something else you wanted me to do before I started setting up the electric fence in the south pasture?"

Wyatt looked at Ashley and raised his eyebrows, getting ready to ask if she was willing to have him bring her horse over to get reacquainted with his former surroundings. She saw the intent in his body language and spared him the awkwardness. "If you two are willing to brave a possible confrontation with The Prince, I'll come along, too."

"Do you have all your tack up at your place?" Tucker asked.

Ashley frowned at him with feigned exasperation, then nodded. "Where else would I keep it?" True, she'd never had a younger sibling, but Tucker was definitely little brother material. This was going to be a cool way to spend the summer. *And maybe longer!*

"B-b-bring up The Frog, then," Wyatt said, then went back and shut all the gates.

"Wow! What did you do? The gates used to be so noisy."

"Wire b-b-brushed the hinges then greased them. They d-d-don't need painting 'caused they're galvanized b-b-but they're sure quiet now."

"That's one of the things that spooked The Prince, that high-pitched grating noise." Ashley turned around when she heard the motor approach her. "What's that thing for?"

"Hop on," Tucker said. "It's what we call The Frog. It's actually a Gator, but it looks more like a frog, crossing wet spots and all. Besides, it's more fun to say you're riding on the back of a frog than a gator. That could be dangerous."

Wyatt held Ashley's hand as she situated herself on the rear-facing bench seat on the back, then let go and stepped over the trailer hitch and sat beside her, thigh-to-thigh. "I figured I wouldn't go cheap on the important stuff, like my back and shoulders. This will save a lot of wear and tear on my body. I could have bought a used four by four utility vehicle, but this one has a warranty, so most repairs will be covered…if it needs them. The trailer is just the right size for a bale of hay or a saddle. Most of the units were like a truck with a bed, but I went for this personnel-carrier style with a trailer. If I'm showing prospective clients around, this would be better than wearing them out before they've even had a chance to see the horses. Plus, if I have my way with the BLM, I'll set aside a certain number of horses to be trained for para-riders. This will be invaluable in getting them from point A to point B."

"That's an awesome plan. Do you have the proposal

written out or is that part of my new job?"

Wyatt blushed with guilt. "Well, I have an outline with all the key points I want to make, but I don't have the words put together in a proposal yet." He looked up. They were at Ashley's home, but Tucker was waiting patiently for him to finish his conversation. Yet another reason to like the kid: good manners and the knowledge of knowing when to shut up. There was a good chance he knew when to speak up, too.

Wyatt looked around, as if he just realized where he was. "Well, just point us in the right direction and we'll load up the tack. Do you mind if I walk him to the stables or do you want to go, too?"

Ashley stretched one arm up in the air then twisted away from Wyatt and pointed her heels. "I could use the exercise, but I would feel better if you walked beside me. I'm still a little skittish about walking on the road by myself after that car spooked me into the ditch. If someone startles The Prince, I don't know if I could handle him by myself."

Wyatt turned away and got out. "D-d-done deal!"

"His tack is in that shed," Ashley said, and pointed up the hill.

"I got it, Boss, if you want to go get acquainted with The Prince."

Wyatt gave him a thumbs up, then offered his arm to Ashley. It wasn't a flirt, but the hill was steep. He'd do the same for any woman, weak or strong. His father brought him up to be a gentleman. He'd keep up the legacy for his own sons…*Gulp! You just told yourself this wasn't a flirt! Stop enjoying her company so much. Save the dreaming for your alone time or you'll wind up embarrassing yourself.*

"Here he is: The Prince," Ashley said breaking his introspective self-admonishment.

"Wow! He's beautiful. How'd you afford such a magnificent creature? Oh, I'm sorry. That was rude…"

Ashley laughed as she shook her head, trying to erase Wyatt's embarrassment with her attitude. She slipped her arm out from under his hand and walked up to the tall, proud horse. "They said he was untamable, but I could tell they just didn't understand him."

Ashley pulled an apple out of her smock pocket and offered it to The Prince. "I had an apple in my pocket that day, too. I'd seen a post about him and couldn't believe it. There was a man on the other side of the valley who said he had a horse that was too wild to keep. I guess it had kicked his favorite dog in the head. The dog was tough and only needed a few stitches, but even that was too much for that wannabe rancher. He said the horse came with the ranch when he bought it. He wanted to clear the pasture but couldn't get a tractor in the gate without the horse attacking it or anyone on it. He took one look at me and scoffed. 'I was going to sell him for $500 but you can have him for free if you get him out of here.'

"Oh, he didn't know me!" Ashley looked over at Wyatt, now standing beside her as she stroked The Prince's forehead. "And you haven't had a chance to know me yet, either, but I'll tell you right now, I love a challenge. And this stuffed shirt had just challenged me big time." She pulled another apple out of her pocket. "Besides, I had wanted my own horse since…" She paused, then looked around, her focus stopping at the evergreen in front of her house. "Since that tree was a seed in a pinecone. I walked up to this magnificent coal black creature, caught the wild look in his eye, and started talking to him, like he was a scared child afraid to come down from the top of a slide in the park. I kept talking as I got closer to the fence. He got closer, too. At least he did until Stuffed

Shirt put his hand on my shoulder and told me to stay back, that the horse was a devil horse."

The Prince's temperament changed when she told the story, reliving the agitation she had felt at the time. She cooed to him and started stroking his muzzle again. "It's okay, baby. I'm just telling Wyatt about the day we first met. He's a good person, too." She turned to Wyatt and gave him the apple. "Give him this and talk softly to him. Let him hear the kindness and sincerity in your voice. These guys may have brains the size of a walnut, but their souls are as big as their back ends."

"Hey, b-b-buddy. Do you want to come stay at m-m-my place for a while? I have lots of fresh spring grass, clean straw in the stables, and a g-g-great exercise area. Pretty soon, I'll be getting some n-n-new students in my school. Maybe you can help me t-t-teach them good manners?"

The Prince nodded his head, repeatedly lifting up Wyatt's empty hand, looking for more apples, but it looked like he was answering the question.

"See, I told you he was smart. Oh, and he likes you, too. Let's walk to the stables. Tucker can bring the saddle in The Frog. If you're walking next to me, The Prince will follow.

Sometimes I think he believes he's taking *me* for a walk when we go out. Besides, this should be easy since he knows where we're going."

Wyatt stepped forward and looked up and down the gravel road before getting on it. "Isn't this d-d-dangerous?" he asked, then took one of the reins.

"If you mean cars, no—not usually. Because of the acoustics of the hills and curve of the road, you can hear a car or truck long before you need to step aside." She grimaced, then added, "Unless it's an electric car and going twice the speed limit." She held up her elbow. "I've endured lots of scrapes and bruises, but having my shoulder dislocated was especially rough."

"Well, maybe I can run the brush hog down here and widen the shoulder on the road some." *Whoa! You didn't stutter! You're not touching her, but both of you are holding onto The Prince's reins. It's like you're touching her through him. This is some eerie stuff. Cool and fantastic, but still eerie.*

"See, it takes less than three minutes to get here. I don't think you should try to work him until he gets reacquainted with this place, though. So, do you want him to graze out back or bring him into a stall?" Ashley asked.

"How about we send him out into this pasture, both of us leading him through the gate together. I'd like him to get more familiar with me, build a rapport. I don't have a horse of my own and will need an older, tame horse to use when I gentle the newbies."

Ashley led the way through the gate, her deep frown worrying Wyatt who was a step behind her. "Are you all right?" he asked.

"I was just trying to figure out what you said." She pulled the last apple out of her pocket and handed it to Wyatt.

"Thanks." He offered the fruit to The Prince. "Here you go, buddy," and ran his fingers through the lock of hair on the gelding's forehead. "The words may sound foreign to you, but I think you're familiar with the technique. Gentling is also called gentle breaking. You're winning the horse over with love and tenderness, not making him submit to your will. No one—whether an animal with two legs or four—wins when it's a domination match. Besides, he's a lot bigger than I am."

"And a lot meaner, I bet," Ashley added. "And the newbies: you're talking about the mustangs you and Tucker want to bring in from the BLM corrals, right?"

Toot! Toot! Toot-toot-toot!

The Prince reared up on his back legs and pawed the air with his front hooves at the shrill honking, then took off to the back of the pasture, his reins trailing behind him.

"Oh, no!" Ashley cried, then turned to chase him.

Wyatt wrapped his arm around her shoulder and grabbed the fence post, penning her in and stopping her from proceeding. "No! Wait! He'll be fine. Give him a chance to calm down by himself."

"But, but..." she cried, her tears of frustration and anger spilling over. She put her head into Wyatt's shoulder and wiped her tears on his plaid cotton shirt. This was her baby and some jerk had upset him.

"He'll be fine," he said. "I promise.'

"Don't you two look cozy?" purred Kimmie.

Chapter 10
Kimmie the C Word

Ashley realized she was clutching Wyatt, remembered that he wasn't hers to hold, then quickly backed away.

Wyatt felt the loss of her warmth, both emotional and physical, then focused on the creator of the brouhaha that had sent The Prince scampering, possibly erasing the confidence he had barely started to create with the high-strung equine.

This was a nightmare. It had to be. He bit the inside of his cheek and winced. No such luck. She was back in his life, at least for right now.

Kimmie the Cutest—or so she thought.

Kimmie the Crassest—or so the teachers called her behind her back

Kimmie the Cruelest—what she was to him and just about every other 'non-perfect' person in her realm.

How in the hell did she ever find him?

And why would she *want* to find him?

The bleach blonde vixen slowly exited her little silver

Prius, one long leg held out, sandaled-toe pointed, then the other. She moved in ultra-slow motion to stand up, her bottom lip pouched out as she coyly brushed an invisible hair out of her face. "Well, aren't you going to give me a kiss hello?" Kimmie asked.

Wyatt glared at her as she made her movie star entrance, unable to take his eyes off the wicked witch who had made his school years so miserable. "Wh-wh-what are you doing here?" he asked, suddenly wishing his linguistic stabilizer was at his side. He looked over and saw that Ashley had retreated to the area of the fence under the tree and was almost cowering.

No, she wasn't cowering. It looked as if her muscles had given out and she was trying to stand up straighter, clinging to the metal fence post with both arms, one leg kicked out to the side, uncooperative or unresponsive, it didn't matter. It was useless to her now.

Rather than voice words that he knew would come out stuttered, Wyatt ignored Kimmie's revolting request for a kiss and rushed over to Ashley.

The sharp pain of feeling spurned hit Ashley like a kick to the head coupled with a violent case of food poisoning. She didn't know if she wanted to vomit or pass out, but she did know she didn't want to be here. Her muscles had failed her, though. Again. Stress made her muscle spasms worse. Extreme stress essentially crippled her. There was no way she could walk home, much less leave the driveway. She looked into the pasture and saw The Prince, pacing back and forth at the far end of the fenced off area, nervous as a caged mountain lion in a traveling zoo exhibit.

Could it get any worse?

Yes, it could.

Ashley looked up just as Kimmie intercepted Wyatt. At first glance, she thought the man she cared so much for had been rushing to be at her side, but now it looked like he was heading toward the blonde bitch. At least, one thing was certain: the living life-size Barbie doll had her long legs wrapped around Wyatt like an octopus around a clam, all her limbs enveloping him as if she was trying to crack his shell, her face in his, trying to suck the life out of him through his mouth.

"G-g-get off of me!" Wyatt shouted as he brought his arm up to break her Pilates-strengthened clutch and vacuum-mouthed kiss.

Kimmie stumbled back but didn't lose her balance or her cool. "But, Wyatt, I thought you were fixing this place up for us and all those children you wanted to have," she cooed, then looked over at the miserable pile of work-smock clothed female, the awkward woman her rich eligible bachelor was rushing toward once again.

"Are you all right, Ashley?" Wyatt asked, his arm around her shoulder.

"That's the woman who knocked me down last month," she whimpered, then sniffed a couple more times and took a deep breath to regain her composure. "She could have killed me but didn't even turn around to see if she'd hit me." Ashley wiped her tears on the sleeve of her smock then looked at Wyatt and glared. "And you're kissing her!" she hissed.

"No, I'm not," he said through clenched teeth, his desire to shout his answer overridden by not wanting Kimmie to see that he and his friend were upset with each other. That was her M.O. Get two friends mad at or upset with each other, then swoop in and take what she wanted, whether a position on the cheer squad or backstage passes to a rock concert.

"I want to go home," Ashley whispered, her neck twitching, causing one shoulder and whole upper body to shudder in spasms.

"Is everything all right here?" Tucker asked, skidding The Frog to a stop in front of Wyatt and Ashley, intentionally blocking the blonde visitor's view of an apparent emotional breakdown with the four-wheel drive vehicle.

"No, it's not all right," Wyatt huffed. "That woman's a trouble maker and has been her whole life. Would you take Ashley home? Make sure she gets settled inside and don't let her stay alone."

Ashley reached up and tried to pull herself up on the crossbar of the gate, but her arm had other plans. It waved in the air, spastically trying to grasp the elusive stationary metal, until she gave up in frustration and let it collapse into her lap.

"Now's not the time to be brave, Ashley," Wyatt whispered close to her face. "I'll explain later. I promise."

Biting her bottom lip to keep a fresh wave of tears contained, Ashley let Wyatt and Tucker shoulder boost her to a standing position, then pivot her into the passenger side of the utility vehicle. Wyatt reached across her lap, stuck his hand between the seat and the back cushion, and fished out the seatbelt, using it to keep her secured.

"Keep hold of her, Tucker, just in case."

Wyatt set his hand on Ashley's shoulder, then gave into his gut and kissed her on the cheek. "I'll see you in a little bit, Angel," he said, then stepped back. "Take care of her, Tucker."

"You bet, I will," he said. He shifted the lever then reached his arm around Ashley, the teenager clutching her to him like an injured cousin.

Wyatt spun around to face Kimmie and found her leaning against her car, her index finger swiping across her phone screen, checking the latest social media comments. She looked up, smiled, and said, "Looks like your little buddy took out the trash. So, are we finally alone?"

"Wha-wha-what are you doing here?" he asked, not taking the bait she was waving in his face: 'Aren't you going to defend your friends?'

"Oh, the boot store in town gave up your address. I told them I had a special delivery for you." Kimmie bent forward at the waist, wiggled her shoulders, then stood up straight again, using her upper arms to push up her new surgically-enhanced breasts. "Do you like them? I had two cup sizes added last fall."

"You'd have been b-b-better off spending it on ch-ch-charm school."

"Oh, Wyatt, you're such a k-k-kick," she said, her lips scrunched up as she mocked his stutter.

Wyatt had never hit a woman, and he didn't plan on doing it now, but he felt his fists curl up of their own volition. He took a long slow, temper-adjusting breath, then fixed his eyes on hers. He realized that he had been taking slow, determined steps toward Kimmie this whole time and was now looking down at her, inches away, her eyes wide in shock and visible shaking giving him a power and confidence he'd never felt before. "Go. Away. Now."

"You'd better not hurt me. I have lawyers and they'd love to make your life miserable," she squeaked, her voice thin and high with fear as she scrambled to open her car door.

"You're trespassing," he said, his voice uncharacteristically low, his eyes still focused on her, as if they were lasers, boring a hole through the middle of her forehead.

Kimmie put the convertible in reverse, spun it around, then put it in drive and hit the accelerator, the click of shifting gears nearly drowned out by the sound of rocks and gravel being kicked up by the tires.

Once she was at the bottom of the driveway and felt safe, Kimmie turned around and screamed, "I'll get you, Wyatt! And your freaky little friends, too!"

***

Wyatt checked the gates, made sure The Prince had settled down, then went back to the house and the stables and locked the doors. *There's no way she can get all this, is there? And what would she want with this little bit of classic country out in the middle of nowhere? Why me?*

Satisfied that all was secured, Wyatt grabbed a bottle of water and headed down the driveway, intending to check on Ashley. Was it too soon? *Nope. Even if there wasn't a possibility that she had hurt herself physically, she was still emotionally battered. Those wounds were harder to see than scrapes or scratches. And took longer to heal.*

At the edge of the road, Wyatt watched as a car with Florine and an older gentleman drove past him and up into Ashley's driveway. *Hmm. Better let Tucker handle this. If Grandma's back, I don't want to show up and get Ashley all riled up again and endure an embarrassing confrontation. It's better to let her calm down by herself. Tucker will call if he needs help. He's good with settling upset horses and little sisters. He'll probably find the right way to deal with Ashley's anger, too.*

Chapter 11
The Frate

"Is there anything else I can do for you?" Tucker asked, handing Ashley a drink of water in the plastic cup with a screw-on lid he had found.

She took a long pull on the straw, glad that her favorite cup was on the counter and the first one he saw so she didn't need to ask him to search for a container that wouldn't spill. She nodded her head, and he pulled the drink away and set it on the counter. "No, I don't need anything else."

"Yes, you do," he said, then grabbed a fistful of paper towels and wet them. "If your hands have calmed down, you need to wash your face."

Ashley lifted her hand to grab the towels, but her reach was erratic; her hand flew up and smacked her chin, causing tears of frustration to start all over again.

"Let me take care of this," Tucker said. "I used to do it for my little sister all the time." He bent to work, wiping the streaks of tears, road dust, and grass pollen from her face. He was just finishing inspecting his work when the door opened, and Florine and a handsome gray-haired man walked in.

"Who are you and what are you doing in my house? With my granddaughter!"

Tucker pulled back and stammered, trying to explain himself, but Ashley spoke up and spared him the embarrassment.

"This is Tucker. There was an incident down at the stables and he helped bring me back here."

"So why is he up in your face?"

Ashley, trying to find a way to talk around the incident without revealing that she had been crying, realized that Grandma was all dressed up, wearing leather pumps instead of boots or tennis shoes, and even had on lipstick and mascara.

"My hands didn't work, so he was wiping off the dirt for me. Tucker works with Wyatt." Now it was Ashley's turn to take the lead. "So, who did you bring in and why are you all dolled up?"

Florine's face reddened with a mix or embarrassment at being called out for wearing makeup and dressy clothes and anger that something so bad had happened that a stranger had to be called in to care for Ashley. While she flustered and sputtered, "Because, well, I, um," her gentleman friend spoke up.

"Maybe you don't remember me. I'm Dr. Stan Williams. I met your grandmother when she brought you in with a dislocated shoulder a month ago. How's it doing, by the way?"

Ashley took a deep calming breath as she realized she had caught her grandmother going out on a date. *It's about time you got a life, Grandma!* The relief relaxed her anxious muscles as no chemical or drug could. She reached her arm up and out, showing off her range of movement.

"Looking good," he said, his cheeks showing a slight pink of discomfiture.

"I just came back for my purse. I thank you for helping Ashley, er…um…young man, but I think it's time for you to leave," Florine said.

Tucker glanced over at Ashley but didn't move or say a word other than, "The name's Tucker." *Wyatt said not to leave her alone. If you're leaving, I'm staying.*

Dr. Williams looked at his watch and cleared his throat.

Florine turned to see what he was hinting at, then flushed

as she remembered. "Oh, shoot. We're going to be late."

"These two seem to be responsible. I'm sure Ashley doesn't need a chaperone."

Ashley looked at Tucker, ten years her junior and barely old enough to shave. "Chaperone? Tucker? Oh, come on, Grandma. We're not romantic. We're just going to chill this evening. You know, popcorn and a movie. Go out and have a good time."

"You're sure you'll be okay?" she asked, looking at Ashley.

"I'll be fine," Tucker answered with a nervous chuckle.

Florine shook her head in defeat. Ashley was stubborn and made her look like a pushover in comparison. If she wanted this kid to hang out and watch movies with her, she'd wind up getting her way, whether she stayed home with her or not. Besides, the girl had a major crush on Wyatt. This kid was just that: a kid. She was probably safer with him in the house than alone. "Well, you two have a good time." She paused, then added, "But not too good."

Tucker blushed, and Ashley rolled her eyes and said, "You, too!"

The door shut behind the older couple as Florine went on her first fancy date since the month before she took on

Ashley as her dependent, nearly twenty-five years to the day dateless.

"The symphony waits for no man or woman," the doctor said.

"I know. I'm sorry. It's just I've been responsible for her for so long, it's hard to stop being the mother hen."

"From all I've seen and what you've told me about Ashley, you did a great job in bringing her up to be a responsible person. I'm glad we got caught. I didn't like sneaking around. It's not as if you need her permission to go out. I saw the relief on her face. She's glad you're dating again."

Florine chuckled softly, a smile brightening her already content face. "She's not the only one. Then again, I'm glad I waited for the right guy. You always seem to find the right thing to say, Stan."

"It's because you're inspirational, Florine. Now, let's talk about Prokofiev. I missed out on fine arts studies in college. I'm so glad that was your passion. I feel as if I have a virtual tutor at my side who also gives good neck rubs."

Florine reached up and used her thumb to press circles into the top of his spine. "After the symphony and a light dinner or dessert, we can stop by your place for a more thorough job." She picked up her purse and blushed. "I made sure I put massage oil in here."

Stan returned her blush. "So that's why you wanted to go back home..."

"You're right. Ashley's an adult and will be fine tonight. Besides, my curfew days expired years ago. I have massage oil, and as you said, I know how to use it."

***

"Let's talk," Tucker said.

"About..."

"Ashley, you had a major meltdown just a few minutes ago. I don't know much about your physical problems, but I'd say that when you get upset, that's when whatever it is overtakes you, then your muscles stop working. You were fine until that bimbo showed up."

"Yes, you're right. Stress makes all the involuntary movements worse. And, I don't know if you noticed or not, but when I saw that my grandmother was dating someone—a decent guy like the doctor who attended me last month—I was relieved. Shoot, I was actually happy, positively ecstatic, but I toned it down, so I didn't embarrass her. That happiness was like a shot of muscle relaxant without the dopey-head side effect."

"Does this mean you'll be able to come back to work with Wyatt tomorrow?"

"Hmph!" Ashley turned away and looked at the bookcase full of DVDs. "What kind of movie do you want to watch?" she asked. "Beauty and the Beast?"

"Who's Beauty in this situation, Ashley, and who's the Beast? He didn't do anything wrong and you know it. Shoot! I've never seen him so ticked, and I've known him for ten years, at least!"

"Despicable Me?" Ashley asked, ignoring him. Maybe he was right, but she didn't want to admit it.

"Yes, you were despicable, Ashley. When you yelled at him, wouldn't look at him, blamed him for someone else's ugliness, it was you being despicable, not him."

Ashley stood up and walked over to the bookcase, her muscles back to their normal slightly erratic behavior rather than unresponsive. "How about How to Train Your Dragon?"

Tucker grunted in frustration, then made a bold decision. He moved next to her, grabbed her by the shoulders and spun her around, then shut his eyes and planted a hard, unemotional, tight-lipped kiss on her mouth.

"Ugh!" Ashley stumbled backwards and landed in the only comfortable chair in the room. "Why'd you do that?"

"Yeah, it was awful, huh? And you didn't want it or expect it, huh? And you'd rather I didn't do it, but there it is: unwelcomed and irreversible." He wiped his mouth with the back of his hand and groaned, "For both of us."

"Then why'd you do it?"

"Good grief, Ashley!" he screeched in frustration. "Don't tell me you don't get it!"

Ashley wiped her mouth with the hem of her shirt, then looked up. "Yeah, I get it. And you're right, both about being unwanted and unforgettable. I'm glad—sorta—that you got me to see reason. You could have explained it all day for a month of Tuesdays, but that kiss...ugh! No offense, I'm sure it would have been fine if you were kissing someone you actually *wanted* to kiss, and she wanted it, too, but to have it just slapped across my face like that..."

"So, you're going back to work tomorrow and we're all cool? I mean, him for getting kissed and me for my desperate act of getting you to see reason?"

"Yeah, I guess so."

"Cool," Tucker said and picked up the fallen DVD of How

to Train Your Dragon. "I can see the microwave. Just tell me where the popcorn is. I'll put in the movie, and we can have our frate."

"Popcorn is in the cabinet to the right of the microwave. And what's a frate?"

"A frate is a friend date. Just because I kissed you doesn't mean I like you for anything more than a friend."

"Oh, please, Tucker. Please, please never mention that kiss again."

"No worries there, A." He grabbed a package of microwave popcorn out of the cabinet, used his teeth to start the tear and ripped off the cellophane, then pushed a few buttons, setting the revolving tray in motion. "And we might learn a few tricks from this movie about taming some of these dragon-related BLM horses. Who thought that the U.S. government and Bureau of Land Management would ever be in the horse-trading business?"

"Not me, but I'm glad they are. Not only are the horses getting new homes, but new generations of people will be able to own and enjoy these fabulous creatures on a one-to-one basis and at an affordable cost."

Tucker brought Ashley her cup of water. "You'll want this,

Cousin. Oh, and only one movie tonight for me because Wyatt and I are going to Hines in the morning with the trailer. Our first load of horses is ready for us. You'll need to get together a list from all the applications submitted—phone numbers, whether or not they have their own trailers, and how much pasture and property they have available—pretty much a spreadsheet, so we can match the horses with the best homes. Sounds like you'll have your hands full tomorrow, Miss Administrative Assistant!"

Ashley sunk back into the Naugahyde recliner. "What did I get myself into?"

"Just like me, it's a labor of love," Tucker said. "You'll love every good day and tolerate the bad ones, glad that you're making a difference in the world of men and horses."

"And women."

"And women," Tucker agreed. He pulled out two large bowls from the drainer on the counter and filled them with popcorn. "Enjoy!"

Ashley pulled the lever on the side of the chair and kicked out the footrest portion. "I already am."

***

"Shoot! I overslept!" Ashley rolled out of bed and stumbled

to the kitchen. "Why didn't you wake me up, Grandma? It's almost ten o'clock?"

"You were finally sleeping soundly, so I didn't want to disturb you. I knew there was some big kerfuffle yesterday afternoon that you didn't want to talk about. When I came in last night, you were tossing and turning something fierce. I called Wyatt at seven and told him you weren't feeling well and wouldn't be coming in today."

"You what?"

"Calm down," Florine said. "He told me not to worry. If you felt better, you could come in later, but he wanted to make sure you took care of yourself. He said you had a key and knew what needed to be done. Something about applications and spreadsheets. Anyway, he and Tucker had to leave right away to get to Hines by noon. Did you know they were getting their first load of horses today? Oh, of course you knew that. You're the secretary."

"Administrative assistant, and yes. It's just that I forgot about it." She sighed, recalling Wyatt being kissed by the blonde bimbo, then felt uncomfortable, ugly and inadequate all over again. "Some things I remember and some things I'd rather forget about. Too bad they don't always wind up in the right columns. I'll take a quick shower and go in. The work won't get done by itself."

By 10:30, Ashley had made the three-minute walk and was at the stables. Looking over the forms sent in from all over the state, and a few from out of state, would be good distraction. There's no way she was going to stay at home, leaving herself open to her grandmother's inquiries about why she had been so upset the day before. Even if there was something she *needed* to do at home, she wanted to be near her horse. She wouldn't be able to ride him because she needed help to get up on him, but he was still her unofficial therapy horse. Just talking to him, touching his coarse hair and solid bulk, smelling his earthy musk, always made her feel better.

"How's it going, my Prince Charming? How about a selfie?" She turned her back to him, snapped a quick photo with her smartphone, then gave him the rest of her apple. "Sorry, I ate some of it. It was my brunch. I didn't feel like eating a real breakfast." She ran her fingers through the hair on his forehead, removing a few pieces of broken grass, glad that he was warm and real, hers for as long as he lived. Yes, she had fantasized about Wyatt, hoping that their relationship would blossom beyond boss and employee, but she had to stop doing that. He wasn't hers to lust after. She shouldn't even emotionally invest in him as a hope or a dream. She'd stick to horses and spreadsheets. They were less likely to hurt her.

Toot! Toot! Toot, toot, toot!

The hairs rose on the back of Ashley's neck at the sound of the familiar automobile horn, knowing who was behind it. She didn't even try to stifle her groan of intense emotional pain but clutched closer to the cross bar on the gate and began her yoga breathing regimen, hoping to calm her rage and therefore any spasms, before they began.

"Have you seen Wyatt?" Kimmie shouted, her icy tone sending shivers up Ashley's arms.

"He's not here," Ashley said, not even turning around to look at her. *One-one thousand, two-one thousand, three-one thousand...* Ashley mentally counted, marking the time she would have to exist in this woman's presence.

Ashley heard the car door open and shut, then the sound of dainty footfalls on the gravel path towards her. "Well, then, would you take this box and give it to him?" Kimmie asked, her tone harsh, like a prison warden addressing an inmate.

Kimmie shoved the bottom edge of the pink milk crate into Ashley's shoulder, punctuating her request. *Such an ugly waste of space! Why would he even allow such a mess on his estate?*

Ashley flinched away. She didn't want anything to do with this woman, but this wasn't her property and she couldn't demand that she leave. She didn't even want to talk to her but did look over her shoulder to see what it was that was so important that *she* would come back to deliver it. She couldn't help but gasp when she saw it. Visible through the sides of the open-style crate were magazines covered with nude couples—busty women and broad-shouldered men in suggestive poses—and what looked like sex toys burgeoning out over the top.

"Maybe this will help him remember all the good times we had *exploring* each other's bodies. Tell him I'll be back tonight to celebrate the anniversary of our first time together."

By staying still, her hands still clutching the fence rail, Ashley refused to accept the box. She didn't—couldn't—say anything, too stunned at the personal nature of the contents and the casual way the buxom blonde in short shorts was trying to pass them off to her. She couldn't do anything but stare, her head moving back and forth in disbelief.

Empowered by the weak woman's shock, Kimmie began her well-rehearsed dissertation. "Yes, Wyatt and I have a long and exciting past. At first, we decided it was best to just have sex all the time, no commitments to each other. We both loved to…well, I won't go into lurid details and embarrass you, but know that Wyatt is quite the adventurer in the bedroom. Or any other place he decides to satisfy our needs."

Kimmie patted her flat tummy. "Of course, now that I'm in a family way, that's going to change. He promised me when he refused to use a condom that he'd take care of me for the rest of my life if I ever got pregnant. He left so soon yesterday, I didn't get a chance to tell him the good news. I decided to send some of our favorite toys ahead for our celebration. You see, it was him, not me, who wanted a family. I think he got me pregnant on purpose." Kimmie smoothed her hand over her ear, tucking a tress of hair behind it. "He always told me how perfect I was, a natural blonde with perfect body proportions and impeccable taste. I'm sure he'll be ecstatic to hear the news."

Even though it was a possibility this woman was lying, her

words still stung. Just hearing about Wyatt being intimate with this witch felt like someone had stabbed a knife into the soft spot in her throat and was now pulling it down, splitting her breast bone, her guts spilling out one organ at a time. *Stop thinking about it! She's a liar! And even if there is a shred of truth in it, that's not who he is now. Tucker would have warned you. Ignore her. Reacting to her words is only going to empower her…*

"Hello?" Kimmie said, shoving the crate into Ashley's shoulder again, trying once more to get her to take the box of intimidation.

Ignore her! Pretend she's an apparition, a ghost of a horrid past. Maybe she'll go away if you don't respond.

"Aren't you going to take his goodies." Kimmie threw back her head and laughed nervously. This wasn't going as she had planned. "Well, these aren't his *real* goodies, but one of the toys is *huge,* just like Wyatt. We used to… Oh, I shouldn't kiss and tell."

Ignore her! She's scared now, making up obvious lies, laughing nervously. Ashley allowed a sliver of a grin to emerge. *This is a waiting game and I'm going to win! Let's see what lame tactic she comes up with next. Turn the time table against the bitch! Who's the fool now? Standing on crushed rock in high-heeled sandals, carrying a box of sex toys, trying to pass it off to someone, anyone… Oh, how sweet it would be for the mail carrier to come by now.*

"I'm going to leave this box right here and take off. Make sure you tell my dear sweet Wyatt that his Kimmie came by and will be back tonight to celebrate being in a family way."

Ashley took a deep cleansing breath, as if this whole time she had been sitting at the gate meditating, then grasped the gate rail and stood up, ignoring the petulant female three feet away. *You've won! You didn't let her get under your skin! This overgrown toddler with perky boobs has been throwing a temper tantrum to get attention and by ignoring her, you won and she lost! Get to work and pretend she never was here.*

Ashley's slight grin turned into a full smile as she ambled to the stables, humming random notes, trying to find just the right song to irritate the pest in the silver electric car. Suddenly, the words flew out at high volume. "Everything's going my wa-ay!" *Let her suck on those words for a while!*

Kimmie grasped the crate closer, ready to drop the suddenly heavy container but not wanting to accept defeat.

She'd make that woman with the awkward gait accept this one way or the other.

Ashley unlocked the door to the stables, slipped inside, then quickly locked it again, dead-bolting it, just to make sure it was secured.

Smack! Smack! Smack!

And there it was. The woman who called herself Kimmie was pounding on the steel door, trying to get her to unlock it. *Nope! She's still the invisible woman to me! Man, this feels good, not letting others get under my skin. Why didn't I figure this out years ago?*

"If you don't open this door, I'm going to call the cops," Kimmie shouted.

Wow! She's desperate. Let her call them. I'll tell them how the owner told her to leave his property yesterday. Ashley looked at her watch. Not even 11:00 yet. Wyatt was still on the road to Hines. He wouldn't be back until late tonight at the earliest; later in the day tomorrow was more likely. She'd have to perform the sergeant at arms aspect of her admin assistant duties pretty soon if this bimbo didn't leave.

Ashley reached up and turned on the radio, blasting her favorite Alice Cooper CD. "You're nothing but tra-ash!" came out the speakers. *Oh, yeah… Sing it!*

"Bitch!" Kimmie screamed through the door, then hit it again, bruising her hand for sure this time. "You're nothing but a broken down…"

Ashley kicked up the volume two more notches, drowning out the slurs from the frustrated female. Then she remembered the last upgrade Wyatt had made to the building: the security cameras. She turned on the computer monitor and watched as Kimmie shoved the pink box of sex paraphernalia next to the doorway then headed back to her car, the convertible top down, affording her a view of the frustrated woman's scowl. It looked like she was giving up. *Phew! It's about time! Can you imagine what would have happened if you had engaged in a shouting match with her?*

"She may have shooed me away for a while," Kimmie crooned as she pulled to a stop at the bottom of the driveway, "but I'll be back later with my little friends, Ar and Son," She stopped, then grabbed her phone and pressed the icon for her friend Barbie.

"Hey, Kimmie! How's it going? Have you got hooked up with W-w-wyatt yet?" Barbie asked. "And if you're driving, just remember to make sure you're on speakerphone."

119

Kimmie pressed the button on the dash, transferring the call to the Bluetooth speakers. "I'm not on the road yet, but I need to get a plan going. If I need to take notes, I want to be parked. I don't want to make that mistake again. Of course, if I hadn't crashed the Beemer, I never would have talked my way into this sweet ride. Hey, remember how you torched that old house and got a boatload of insurance money out of it?"

"Of course, I remember," Barbie answered. "Why do you want to know about that? I thought you liked where you're living now."

"Not my place, sweetie, but Wyatt's. His place is ancient. I think it's some historic monument or something. The guy at the Boot Barn who told me where it was said Wyatt's spent a ton of money on renovating this place, but it still looks like a dump to me. If—I mean, when—I get him to marry me, I don't want to live in squalor. It might be faster to burn this place down and start from scratch. Of course, if there isn't a home to stay in, then I'll have to take an extended vacation while he builds me another one. And the way Wyatt is, all hands on, a 'gotta make sure it's done right so I'll supervise it' kind of guy, that means I can go to Greece or wherever without him. Are

120

you game?"

"Game to help you burn the place down or go to Greece?" Barbie asked.

"Both, but since you're out of town right now, and I want to get this done right away, just tell me what I need to do, and I'll do it myself."

"First off, you have to make sure you don't use something as a fire starter that isn't native to the building."

"Huh?"

"If there's a lawnmower around, you can use gasoline to start a fire on it, but don't use lighter fluid of something like that that wouldn't normally be found outside. If the place has old wiring, you could strip some wires and cause it to short out, but I think that's beyond your skill set," Barbie said, hoping she wasn't insulting her friend. She might need her in the future. Bimbos like Kimmie were handy to have around at times but were prone to being vicious if payback time ever arose.

"How about I just pour gasoline over the lawnmower and torch it?"

"It wouldn't work unless it was inside the house. And why would it be inside the house? No, tell me more about the layout."

"There's a barn. I can see the lawnmower parked outside it. If that catches fire and spreads to the barn, maybe the house will burn down, too?"

"Now you're thinking, Kimmie. I say, go for it. Oh, but don't plan our trip to Greece until after June first. I want to be able to get a Mediterranean tan. These fake bake tans are lame. I need at least a Hawaiian tan, but a Greek one would be best."

***

What the hell? Ashley looked at the monitor above her desk, verifying that the feed from the security camera at the gate was being recorded. Arson? Should she call the cops right away or wait until Kimmie put action to her threat? Right now, the grass outside was so green, there's no way it would burn, with or without gasoline poured on it. *Just wait and see if she pulls out more rope to hang herself with.*

"Oh, by the way, Kimmie, I heard through the grapevine that your dear old ex-stepfather made parole early. I guess he had exceptionally good behavior. He's been out for almost a week now."

"Oh, no, no, no. I'll make a few phone calls and have

Sidney Silverstein thrown right back in the slammer. I'm sure I could be suffering flashbacks or something. The story I made up against him was watertight. No amount of good behavior can override my flawless performance!"

"Just wanted to let you know. He's sure to want payback for you lying about the sexual assaults. I'd watch your back if I were you."

"Thanks. I guess I'd rather hear it from you than meet him face-to-face on the streets somewhere. I'll go get a can of gas and some matches and get this party started. I'll let you know how it went this evening."

"No, no, no on the matches, Kimmie. Go get one of those long lighters like they use for starting campfires or fireplaces. If you want Wyatt to get insurance money, it can't look like arson. And if you aren't sure about something, give me a call. I'm here for you, Lady K."

"Thanks, Barbie. You're a true friend." *Click.*

Phone call disconnected, Kimmie wrote 'gas can + long lighter = $$' on the back of her charge card receipt from breakfast. "This shouldn't take long." She turned around and looked at the property, visualizing it without the barn, stables, or the old house, instead sporting a huge southern-style mansion with lawn jockeys and rose trees on the manicured grass in front.

"If all goes well, I should be Mrs. Wyatt Younger before the end of the month. Little baby Younger and I will be on a tour of the Mediterranean Islands while Daddy is building his family a new home. Daddy will be so sad that little baby Younger will never have a chance to grow up." She laughed at the deception she had planned. "That tends to happen to imaginary babies."

Kimmie put the car in drive and decided she'd pick up the gas and lighter from the little market in town rather than go all the way into Monmouth. *Besides, having that baby in high school was one child too many. I can't disappear for six months again. Plus, I never got anything but trouble out of that brat's dad! Make believe babies are much easier to handle.*

***

"Well, th-th-that was easy enough. I'm sure glad they have loading the m-m-mustangs onto trailers down to a science with those chutes," Wyatt said. He walked around his new six-horse trailer one more time, rechecking the hitch, safety chains, and latches on the back to make sure all were securely fastened.

"Did you ever call Ashley?" Tucker asked, making sure his face was out of view so Wyatt didn't see his apprehension.

"I d-d-don't think she wants to talk to me. She was sure m-m-mad last time I saw her."

"Before we leave, I think you ought to reach out to her. She and I had a…a talk last night and I think I made her see the light." Tucker pointed to the phone in Wyatt's pocket. "The call won't cost you an extra dime and you have nothing to lose. My mama said there was nothing sexier than a contrite man."

"S-s-sexy? I'm not trying to be s-s-sexy!"

"No, but you do want to keep your employees happy, right? You'll make her happy, and me at the same time, by calling. Get it over and done with so we can hit the road. I didn't sleep a wink last night in the back of this trailer, even if the floor was showroom clean and they were new sleeping bags."

"Yes, you d-d-did unless you snore when you're awake."

Wyatt started to get in the cab, then sighed in defeat, and pulled out his phone before he chickened out. "Hi, Ashley? Yes, we're okay. We g-g-got six beauties to b-b-bring back.

Hey, I'm sorry f-f-for…"

Wyatt's eyes widened and his words evaporated as he listened to Ashley. "B-b-but you didn't d-d-do anything wrong!"

Tucker watched as a huge grin grew on his boss's face, the anxiety and fear he had when he started the call gone like a soap bubble in the wind.

"All r-r-right. We'll see you in about f-f-five hours or so."

"Well…" Tucker prompted, eager to hear how it went.

"She apologized to m-m-me, so we're g-g-good," Wyatt said, giving Tucker the abbreviated version. *There's no reason to tell him she said that she knew he had better sense than to make out with the witch with a capital B. And if he wanted someone to kiss, he wouldn't have to bring someone in from across the state. Shoot, he could holler across the street and do better than that!*

"I think you'd better be good to that woman," Tucker said. "I think she's sweet on you."

"Well, I'm k-k-kinda fond of her myself." *And that's an understatement!*

Chapter 12
Wedding Day

Six months later, October 24

"Are you sure you want to get married?" Florine asked. "I mean, you and Wyatt have been through a lot in six months, but it's still less than a year that you've known each other."

"You're not going to talk me out of it, Grandma. Besides, you only knew Stan for five months and got married. We're waiting longer than you two."

"Yes, but we'd both been married before and knew what to look for. And what to look out for."

"So, is there something about Wyatt that I should look out for? Is there something wrong with him? If so, why didn't you say something before? Why are you waiting until thirty minutes before the ceremony?" Ashley asked.

"No, there's nothing wrong with Wyatt that I can see. I guess I'm nervous because I still think of you as my little three-pound preemie, fists raised to challenge the world."

Ashley looked down her nose at her grandmother and

snorted. She didn't have to say, 'You always say that,' because after all these years, the 'look' was enough.

"Actually, Wyatt is *too* perfect," Florine said.

"How can a guy be too perfect?"

"He's handsome, rich, has his own place, has a dream job..." Florine said, starting to count Wyatt's assets on one hand, then dropped the veil she was getting ready to pin on Ashley's head so she could continue to enumerate.

Ashley picked up calling out his assets, "Is kind to humans and animals, considerate, generous, a humanitarian, a genius when it comes to gentling wild horses..." She quit bragging about Wyatt and put the veil back in her grandmother's hand. "Admit it. He's about as perfect as Stan except Stan is a genius with gently fixing broken people and Wyatt gently breaks wild horses."

"Oh, all right. Say, I just heard Kimmie got sentenced today. The judge gave her five years for attempted arson and ten years for filing a false police report and bearing false witness, lying about her stepfather assaulting her. Oh, and they are *not* to be run consecutively."

"I'm so glad she was on speakerphone and in a convertible."

"And that Wyatt had those cameras set up and she was crowing about her misdeeds loud enough to be recorded. I don't think I ever told you how happy I was that you didn't start a shouting match with her that day. That whole scenario could have gone so wrong. I don't think she would have attacked you, but you never know."

"I can't believe how stupid she was, trying to buy her arson materials from Harvey's Market. Kathy wrote down her license number on the credit card receipt and called the cops just after you did. Talk about being caught red-handed!" Ashley checked the fit of the veil, then pushed it a little to the left so it was centered, her arm and hand calm.

"I'm just glad that Loren wasn't in uniform when he showed up and was in his own car." Florine pushed the bobby pin into place, securing the veil on that side.

Ashley repeated her favorite part of the story, her face aglow as she related it. "There I was—sitting at my desk, watching the incriminating footage with Loren—when she showed up again. She went right around back to the lawnmower, front and center in the camera's field of view, live as Loren and I watched it. Did I tell you she even held her little pinkie out as she poured the gasoline over the mower, like she was at high tea, sipping a cup of Earl Grey?" She shook her head and chuckled.

"Then Loren came out and caught her. She tried to say she was just washing her fiancé's riding mower as a surprise for him. Geez! Washing it in gasoline?" Florine said, fidgeting with the drape of the veil.

"Of course, having the lighter in her hip pocket wasn't too cool, either. But the best part was her temper tantrum."

"N-n-no," Wyatt said, opening the door the rest of the way, peeking into the room to make sure everyone was ready. He took two steps over to Ashley and put his hand on her shoulder. "The best part was when you sang 'Everything's going my way' at the top of your lungs. That was some hissy fit she threw. Loren told me later that he really enjoyed slapping those bracelets on her."

Florine looked from Ashley up to Wyatt and back again. "You can't be in here. It's bad luck to see the bride before you're married."

Wyatt leaned down and kissed his wife gently on the lips. "She's already my wife, aren't you, dear."

"What?" Florine screeched, then brought it down twenty decibels. "What? You're married already? I thought you were just living together."

"Well, I didn't care about a big wedding and neither did Wyatt, but I didn't want to deny it to you. I know my mother never got married, so you missed out there. I'm more your daughter than she was, or at least I feel that way, so I wasn't going to deny you walking your baby down the aisle...even if I am twenty-six years old."

Florine's eyes misted up and she sniffed back what bypassed her tear ducts and tried to run down her nose. "That's so considerate of you, sweetheart. And you, too, my number one son."

"Our pleasure, Florine, but I think that would be grandson."

"Nope. As Ashley said, she's more my daughter than my daughter was, God rest her soul, so I'm claiming you as my son."

"That works for both of us, I'm sure. Mom." Ashley stood up, long white gown flowing around her, and gave 'Mom' a big hug. "Now, since everyone in town is here, plus half the folks from Wyatt's hometown, too, let's get this show on the road."

"Other Mom, would you join my first mom out there? I'd like a minute or two alone with my wife, or as everyone else believes, my fiancée."

"All right. It's not as if you need a chaperone." Florine took one more look in the mirror, wiped away a smudge of mascara, then left the room. Her once imperfect life was now ideal. *Thank You, Lord!*

"Ashley, you know I love you, but I don't think I ever told you how proud I am of you."

"For what?"

"For everything. You've always been there for me, making sure everything was in order, then saved my buildings from being burned to the ground, showed me a few tricks about gentling the mustangs so they only needed half as much attention, but..."

Ashley leaned forward, waiting to hear the rest of the story. When he remained mum, she prompted him with a shoulder nudge and a mild chastisement. "You know we have people waiting for us, right?"

He nodded and continued. "But the most important reason I love you is that you trust me. That day when Kimmie came, ready to tear everything I had apart with her malicious lies and," he shook his head, remembering the pink box that was still on the property when he returned the next day, "her lies and her props. I've seen her work before. She tried to ruin my brother, too. She told everyone they were together for three years, but they never even went out on a date—they were just in the same drama classes. In school, she'd make a show of walking in front of him, pretending he was being a gentleman, opening doors for her when he was just trying to get rid of her. The only peace anyone in school got was when she disappeared at the end of her junior year then came back at Christmas her senior year. She tried to hook up with Colton again, but by then, he was out—out of the closet. She looked so lame, trying to cuddle up to him when he only had eyes for Jim. By the way, Colton said to give you this."

Wyatt gave her a kiss on the cheek. "He and Jim missed their flight. They'll be here for the reception tonight, though."

"Knock, knock," Stan said. "Are you ready, you two? The quartet's played every song they know twice and now the crowd is calling for the Wedding March."

Wyatt stood up, reaching for Ashley's hand. "Here's to trust, love, and companionship," he said.

"Good friends and plenty of homes for all the wild horses we can tame."

"And Tucker has The Prince ready Wyatt to walk you

down the aisle," Stan said. "It's going to be a perfect wedding."

"And a perfect life," Ashley and Wyatt said together.

"And a perfect life," Stan agreed. "Just like mine and Florine's."

THE END

A Note from the Author

Thank you for reading *Be My Angel,* one of my few stand-alone stories. At least for now. You never know if Wyatt and Ashley will be back with more adventures, helped along by the young and resourceful Tucker.

I'd appreciate it if you took a moment and left a review on Goodreads and/or Amazon. Your impressions on the story may help others decide whether this story is a good fit for their tastes.

If you're interested in the other books or projects I'm working on, please sign up for Time Travelers Anonymous (www.danihaviland.com) and follow me on BookBub (http://bit.ly/BBDani).

PREVIEW

Following is a preview of my next release *Time in a Little Blue Bottle*, a novella that ties into some of the characters from The Fairies Saga.

Chapter One
In London
With Elvis and Company

Rare Arts and Antiquities Emporium
January 31, 2015

The academic investigators who practically lived in the Emporium's windowless low-ceilinged room paid no attention to the odd lot of men gathered in the corner. They were passionate about their own studies and didn't have any interest in the long-haired old men in period costumes or the celebrity impersonators who hovered near them.

Suddenly, as if led by an orchestra conductor, everyone in the room looked up—not a mumble or whisper was uttered—then they returned to their hunched-over postures and resumed their research, not knowing or caring what had happened.

But some realized the air was different now, enlivened. The atmosphere of the sub-basement area was now brisk, no longer musty or devoid of energy, but alive, almost electrically charged. A few of the scholars looked around to see what had happened. The others—more intent on their studies—simply sniffed the air for smoke or a gas leak, then returned to their yellowed tomes.

A new patron stood just beyond the old men in the archives section. His tall broad-shouldered stance looked out of place among the others. His arrival down the rickety, threadbare carpeted stairs had not been heard nor seen, but he was certainly the center of attention now for all but the most grizzled academics.

"Wh...why are you here, Cleveland?" Leonardo da Vinci the elder asked, subconsciously pulling his loosely knotted cravat up over his billowy ivory shirt. *Why would the Prime Vampire be here today? Or ever?*

Cleveland smiled at his former protégé. "Do I need a reason?"

The fixation on the tall newcomer wasn't just the result of his sly grin or Olympic swimmer body build. When he spoke, everyone in the musty alcove gazed at him in fascination, as if he was about to share the secret of how to make a million euros without breaking a sweat or a law.

Leonardo cleared his throat and blinked erratically as he tried to erase his nervous smile. "No, no. You're just as welcome here as anyone else. I was just wondering if you needed some help with research. As you know, my associates and I have a lot of experience…"

Cleveland laughed without constraint, causing the young blonde librarian who had been watching the dark-skinned demi-god to drop her armload of papers. She quickly gathered them together, then hid under the work center table to listen in on their conversation.

"No offense, Leo, but I think I have more 'experience' than five of you put together."

"At least," Leonard the elder agreed. "Sorry. I meant no disrespect, sir. That being agreed upon, if there is anything you require, please, do not hesitate to ask."

The full-lipped man with the black pompadour nudged the sixty-ish Southern gentleman next to him. "Who's he, Twain?" he drawled.

"Sakes alive, Elvis, didn't you pay attention? They gave us a whole week of training about Cleveland before we could

138

move up to the next level."

"Um, I must have overslept that week. Or maybe that was just for you folks from the 1800s. We only learned about current, important stuff," Presley said, then ran his fingers behind his ear, making sure he still didn't have a hair out of place.

"Horse feathers! I know they still teach about the vampire who saved—or changed, depending on your point of view—Alexander the Great." The white-haired, but still robust author twisted up the ends of his mustache. "Kids! You buy them books, teach them to read, learn them a job, and still they just lollygag around, dandying themselves up for the ladies."

"Hmph. I'll bet there's nothing he can do that I can't do better," Elvis said, then punctuated his remark with another snort of disgust.

All the other time travelers hurried to 'shush' the impetuous newcomer, but it was too late. Cleveland had heard Elvis.

"Since your education was neglected—and I don't see how they let you out of the primary classes with that attitude—I'll give you a short lesson. I can hear better than any animal around, so be careful what you say, even if you're in the next room; I can see further than any of Galileo's telescopes," he nodded to the 15th century sage at the far side of the round table, "and I can jump higher than any frog in Calaveras County...or any other animal that has ever existed."

Elvis gulped hard but didn't even try to speak.

"But you're right. There's one thing you can do that I can't..." Cleveland paused for effect, then said, "I can't put on mascara."

Elvis pulled his chin in, embarrassed that the secret to his beautiful blue eyes was being so blatantly dismissed.

"You see, I can out-perform any man, past or present; am stronger than any vampire who ever existed; I can even walk in the noonday sun, but I'll be damned if I can see my reflection in a mirror!"

All the men in the area laughed along with Cleveland. The Prime Vampire knew they all feared him, but he'd like to think that he could still make a joke out of his one limitation.

Cleveland turned away to look at the two men across the room, and the nervous laughs stopped abruptly.

"Actually, I'm here for a reason. I need to make sure your short-statured associate doesn't make a mistake with that man," and nodded to the two men seated at a corner table, intent on the contents of a small tin.

"Simon?" asked Michelangelo. "He's harmless. He gets a bit overwhelmed at times, but he means no ill will. He should learn how to defend himself better, though. Just recently—a year or two ago—he was beat up and robbed of his map. He managed to sort it out without any permanent harm done, but he's been a bit skittish ever since."

Cleveland turned his gaze back to the balding genius. "Any permanent harm…yet."

"Oh, no, sir. I promise you. Simon is a crusty sort, but he's just a traveler, and only an observer at that. Oh, and I have no idea who that…that day walker is."

"That, dear Michel, is no day walker. That is Marty Melbourne. He may look inauspicious, but I guarantee you, what transpires between those two will make or break a country. A large country. A water-locked country…"

"You're talking about Australia, aren't you?" Mark Twain asked. "I've been there. It's in no danger. Those folks are a tough bunch."

Cleveland shook his head. "Now *you're* the one talking like a day walker. You were there when? Late 19th century?"

Mark Twain nodded, too angry and embarrassed at Cleveland's righteous admonishment to speak. Australia was a new colony—relatively speaking—when he had first visited it in 1895. He had returned as a time traveler only a few years ago. He still found it hard to believe so much could change in a century. It rarely happened that he thought of time in a linear fashion. He'd been a time traveler for over a hundred years, but occasionally forgot how time—easily bent or pulled aside for travelers like those in his elite group—could be permanently creased or torn, thus causing a rift in the time space continuum and creating an alternate 'now.'

Cleveland returned his attention to Michelangelo. As if he could read his mind—and he could—the tall, dark potential menace answered the scientist/artist's unspoken question. "This man's legacy—the Melbourne Legacy—needs to be protected. You do know what a Möbius strip is, don't you?"

Michelangelo shook his head in frustration, then looked to the most affable in the group for help.

Twain sighed, then rolled his eyes. Time to teach the teacher. Again. He grabbed a strip of paper from the trash next to the copier, gave it a half twist, then taped the joined edges together. "Look, Mike, I'm sure you've seen this before, but it was only recently—relatively so—that it was named." Twain pulled a pen from the cup on top of the printer. He put pen to paper and drew a continuous line. "See? I didn't lift the pen, essentially marking on only one side, but still, I've drawn on both—two—sides."

"And that is the Melbourne legacy. In this timeline—which we must maintain—James Melbourne is born in the 20th century. However, he lives out his life, and makes grand contributions and changes in the 18th century, and eventually dies, in the 19th century. The son of that man—that pushy, busybody Marty Melbourne—*has* to be found and protected by a friendly local, so to speak, after he arrives in Australia with The First Fleet in 1788. We can't let his father find him and bring him back to this time, the 21st century. James Melbourne may have been born to live out his life in this era, but that is not his destiny. Too many lives in Australia—then and now—depend on him *not* returning."

Michelangelo shook his head. *He didn't care what happened to anyone named Melbourne, or to Terra Incognita—or Australia or whatever they called that oversized island now.*

He also didn't care if he was upsetting Cleveland, this

143

statuesque male with the most perfect body he'd ever seen. He was tired of staying alive. Death was part of living, and he had been ready to check out for decades, maybe even centuries: he'd lost track. He'd have gladly succumbed to the peace of death long ago, but Leonardo, Senior kept pushing the Fountain of Youth tonic on him, either blatantly in a toast, or slyly, in his cup of evening wine.

However, if he could get this tribute to the male form to pose for a painting—or maybe indulge him even more on a personal level—he'd be willing to hang around for a few more centuries. It didn't matter to him whether Cleveland was human or vampire. Either way, he was indeed 'prime.'

{End of preview of Time in a Little Blue Bottle}

Other books by Dani Haviland

A Stingray Christmas: (First book in the Arlie Undercover series) Anchorage detective on medical leave travels from Alaska to Arizona to see for the first time the son he'd fathered as an anonymous sperm donor. Great and rotten surprises await the cop with the smartest smartphone around.

The Biggest Heart Ever: (Book two in the Arlie Undercover series) When would Arlie learn that trying to do everything by himself could be deadly—and make Charlene a widow before they were married?

Always a Bigger Fish: (Book three in the Arlie Undercover series) Back in Alaska, Arlie finds out he's a target. Will vacationing detective Billy Burke (from THE FAIRIES SAGA) have information to help nab the scalper?

THE FAIRIES SAGA SERIES
(in order with novellas):

Naked in the Winter Wind: (lengthy novel) How does an older woman wind up as a young hottie in Revolutionary War era North Carolina? First book in the time travel series.

Ha'Penny Jenny: (historical novella) More about the naïve and psychic young girl who was adopted into a time traveling family. Will her past catch up to her?

Aye, I am a Fairy: (lengthy novel) Young British lord finds himself entwined with a time traveling family and must decide if he should go back in time, too. Second book in the series.

Dances Naked: (novel) Directionally challenged time traveler is rescued by Cherokee in 18th century. What must he do before the chief will show him to The Trees, the portal through time?

Chasing Christmas: (historical novella) A young Cherokee is rescued from an abusive man and changes the lives of many in this 18th century America family.

The Great Big Fairy: (lengthy novel) Very tall Benji grew up in the 20th century but was born in the 18th. When he finds a way to return to his grandparents in the distant past, he goes for it. Once there, he realizes he can't stay, but must return to the future. Fourth book in the series.

Little Bear and the Ladies: (historical novella) What's a bachelor trapper to do with all the females he rescues from the Hessian mercenaries? He'd better hurry and figure something!

Little Drummer Boy: (historical novella) Young Scout works to earn money for a home in post-Revolutionary War America but runs up against prejudices and snowstorms.

Never Too Young: (historical novella) Scout and Ha'Penny Jenny have grown up, but will they be able to spend their life together, or will the past and ruffians get in their way?

Time in a Little Blue Bottle: (novella) Bella and her teenage guide are trying to beat Elvis and Mark Twain to the vial of Fountain of Youth elixir. Will they make it?

CONTEMPORARY NOVELLAS

BENJI: THE LOST YEARS

Pool Boy Wanted: No Experience Preferred (rather racy) Young Benji has been a hostage and slave, but life gets worse when an older woman decides she wants him as her own.

Luke the Unexpected: Love of classic motorcycles brought them together, but Luke and Holly have other challenges to face. Find out how their friend Benji got his stripes here.

STAND ALONE NOVELLAS

Kit Kringle: An Alaskan Tale (contemporary) Kay moved to Alaska for the wrong reasons, then decided to stay and start her own business. What she hadn't planned on were prejudices and falling in love.

Three Are One: (contemporary) The post chaplain tried to help the young widow adjust, but would his feelings for her and the search for his lost sister cause problems?

One Arctic Summer: (contemporary) Barrow, Alaska 1994. The touch she never forgot.

Dani Haviland has never been one to believe, "You can't do that!" She started her own business in 1994, selling tractor parts in Alaska, then segued to writing and publishing books, becoming a *USA Today* bestselling author in the process. She currently splits her time between Alaska and Oregon, tirelessly writing and gardening, publishing and promoting, while claiming to be 'retired.'

Contact

Website: www.danihaviland.com

Twitter: @dani_haviland

Facebook: Dani Haviland Author *or* The Fairies Saga Fans

Amazon: http://bit.ly/dhAuthor

BookBub: http://bit.ly/BBDani

Goodreads: http://bit.ly/2DHgdrds

email: dani@danihaviland.com

www.ingramcontent.com/pod-product-compliance
Lightning Source LLC
Chambersburg PA
CBHW082010170626

46817CB00009B/3052